THE APOSTLE

By Martin Otchevnik

After such knowledge, what forgiveness? Think now
History has many cunning passages, contrived corridors
And issues, deceives with whispering ambitions,
Guides us by vanities.

                    T. S. Elliot, Gerontion

This is why I speak to them in parables: Though seeing, they do not see; though hearing, they do not hear or understand. In them is fulfilled the prophecy of Isaiah: You will be ever hearing but never understanding; you will be ever seeing but never perceiving. For this people's heart has become calloused; they hardly hear with their ears, and they have closed their eyes. Otherwise they might see with their eyes, hear with their ears, understand with their hearts and turn, and I would heal them.

              Matthew 13:13-15

But we speak the wisdom of God in a mystery, even the hidden wisdom, which God ordained before the world unto our glory: which none of the princes of this world knew.

          1   Corinthians 2:6-15

HIBERNIA, [110 CE]

They are all gone now, friends and enemies. Yohannon was the last, may he find eternal peace. He was the best of us, though he never accepted me.

Yaakov the Nazirite was Yeshua's brother, *adelphotheos*. Some -- who did not know him – have called him Yaakov the Just. He was condemned in Jerusalem, eight years before Titus' legions came and raised a blood-stench unlike any that had gone before. The mob carried Yaakov to the pinnacle of the Temple and threw him down. When he didn't die, they stoned him, finally crushing his head with a fuller's hammer.

Shimon the fisherman, also known as Cephas: he was Yaakov's confederate in most things. Cephas claimed that Yeshua anointed him as his successor, but this was never true. According to questionable sources, Cephas was crucified upside down. He supposedly said he was not worthy to die in the same manner as Yeshua. Cephas was correct in that assertion, if not in much else. The world remembers him as Petrus.

Most of the others -- Cephas' and Yaakov's backscratchers -- died miserably: Andrew, Cephas' brother, on a cross in Achaea; Yaakov, son of Zebedee, slain by Herod's sword; Philip, crucified by the Romans at Hierapolis. As for Toma, the twin – who knows where his bones may lie? Some say he went east into the unknown countries. Others may also have disappeared in the east: Bartholomaios, sometimes called Natanel; and Yehudah and Shimon, the fiery Zealots. Matthias the tax collector was not a partner to their infamy. If he escaped Titus, he may have gone down into Ethiopia, where he would have preached quietly, as was his way.

They were not central to my lifework, those so-called apostles, though they are revered today in sly contrived legend. I had my own friends and companions: Barnabas, Timothy, Titus, Silas and Aquilla -- and the indomitable women who stood to witness in the churches: Priscilla, Syntyche, Tryphaena, Tryphosa, Phoebe, Junia and Lydia.

As for me, I have been a troubled guest on this shadowy earth. I will soon draw my final breath here in the north, *terra incognita*. Unlike Yohannon, I have had few pupils. I will die alone and be lowered into an unmarked grave. To the local people -- they who are as pallid as their anemic winter sun – I am Cian Oenfer, the ancient lonely one.

Ah, but in Cilicia, more years ago than I can count, how my sisters' sweet voices rang with delight, crying: Saul, Saul. And when I was still a young man, confounded by visions, Maryam Magdala bequeathed me a name that she hoped would keep me humble. Once that name was despised, but now it is strangely venerated -- for opinions I never voiced, and for philosophies I could never have conceived. They call themselves Christians, those who praise me. I am one of their many lost martyrs, Paul, the Apostle.

TARSUS, CILICIA [10-27 CE]

During my long life, I have seldom been unvisited by apparitions. Many say that they long for this fiery gift, but what do they know of pain, confusion, terror – and finally obligation? I remember the first time: I was very small, walking with my family past the temple of Sandon in Tarsus, where I was born. I suddenly screamed and tried to pull away from Father's strong hand. The temple's winged lion statue had come alive above me – I can see it still, rearing, menacing, its talons sharpened and ready for my blood.

After that, the dreams came with great frequency. My mother and sisters took turns sleeping with me; I would awaken in terror, drenched in cold sweat. Even in daytime, if I saw a spider, it was Arachne, whose tale had been recently told by the Roman poet Ovid. Any dog in an alley could become Cerberus, child of Typhon and Echidna -- three mouths with an appetite for meat. I was particularly terrified of being devoured by Chimaera, the lion with a goat-head emerging from its back, and with a long tail ending in a serpent's hissing mouth. Chimaera was said to live in the hills of Lycia, only one day's walk from Tarsus.

I could be anywhere, alone or in company, when suddenly I would find myself rising far above the city, able to see all the way southward to the sea, and as far as Mount Argaeus to the north. Sometimes a powerful wind raced off the mountain, and a great bright cloud, and fire flashing, and lightning emerging from the fire. Vague beings, barely glimpsed, fluttered above and below me; at other times, I was carried aloft by formless slithery entities.

All free residents of Tarsus had been made Roman citizens by Gnaeus Pompeius Magnus when he came in my great-grandfather's time, after crushing the Cilician pirates. We were also nominally Jews, although Hebrew was not spoken in our home. My father made a half-hearted effort to instruct me in the laws and language of our people. I was not an enthusiastic student, nor was Father a dedicated teacher.

I was the only son and so was intended to assume Father's role in society, to learn and eventually oversee his many business interests. But by the time I was seven it was clear that my frightening ways might make this impossible. Despairing, Father sent me to Cleanthes, head of the Stoic academy founded before my birth by Athenodorus Cananites. Athenodorus had been a native Tarsan who served for many years as tutor to the emperor Augustus. Upon his return from Rome, Athenodorus expelled the previous government and wrote a new constitution for our city, establishing Tarsus as a permanent Roman fief. How could I know then that I would one day pass through the remains of the *stoa poikile* in Athens, where Zeno, the distant architect of my teachers' philosophy, had lived and argued?

Only sons of the privileged class could hope to attend Cleanthes' academy, but there was a deeper reason for my admission. Athenodorus had been something of a mystic; he saw signs in everyday affairs. Once, when he was living in Athens, it was said, he had communicated openly with a ghost who was haunting his home. Cleanthes shared his master's interest in magic and sorcery, and so it was that he took on the task of helping me to conquer my visions.

I remember very little of my studies today, but I did manage to gain some recognition in the academy. Learning came by way of debate, which was a strength I have always had, despite a voice that can best be described as reed-thin. By the time I left Tarsus, I had a good basic understanding of Greek and Roman thinking, although I was never a scholar, nor could have been.

Several different schools of thought were popular in those days. Epicureans believed in the system of Democritis – that the world is composed of atoms which combine and recombine in an eternal dance. Epicureans worked at living modestly, seeking a state of tranquility and freedom from fear, as well as absence of bodily pain. They taught that divine beings existed, but that such beings had no concern for humans. Stoics, like Cleanthes and my other teachers, were also atomists, but they denied the existence of any gods: they argued that the primal *Pneuma*, the soul of the world, is intelligent, that it infuses and permeates all discrete things, *logoi spermatokoi*. Some also spoke of Pythagoras, who said that the first entity in existence was the monad, which brought forth the dyads, and then numbers, points and lines. As for Cleanthes, he went one step further, reaching back to Parmenides, who said that the material world is a delusion, that change, plurality and even our own individual selfhood are completely deceptive.

About a dozen boys reclined in a comfortable semi-circle around Cleanthes. I was nervous. Everyone else seemed older, larger, more pleasing in body and countenance.

"The gods were man's constructions," Cleanthes began, "invented to help us find solace in a confusing and frightening world. God or the gods have no meaning except to provide a context for a rational man to become more perfectly ethical, more simply and humbly good."

He smiled broadly, searching each of our faces in turn.

"But this does not mean that there are no gods. Or -- recalling my own master, Athenodorus -- no ghosts. You will someday understand this apparent contradiction."

I remember my stuttering shock. Tarsus was a city of statues, each dedicated to a single different god or goddess. One of the older boys mentioned this.

Cleanthes calmly said that these were all in error: that there must instead be an all-encompassing spirit in the world, as well as absolute, inflexible laws by which events large and small must occur.

"This spirit," he said, "because it is boundless, is unknowable -- and so not a reasonable topic of philosophical discourse. We only seem to exist, in a limited universe of mind and matter. Let us call these attributes: thought and extension. Now consider a being consisting of infinitely more attributes. Add that this being is itself infinite, and that therefore it must permeate us and we it. How can we even begin to contemplate such a being, let alone make guesses about its intentions for us? To think we can converse with this being and argue right or wrong? Sad childish fantasies."

One of the older boys asked about free will. Cleanthes smiled.

"There are laws of order and process," he said, "not understood or understandable by humans. When we seem to be making free choices, we are actually chained to events and circumstances which must adhere to those laws of order and process. There is therefore no free will."

This was shocking to me. Our synagogue held scrolls which told of an angry, jealous, active and unforgiving god, *hakadosh baruch hu* -- The Holy One, Blessed Be He. Always impetuous, I raised my small hand.

"Master, what about the Holy One of the Jews? The law says that he created the world and humans as well."

Cleanthes rubbed his bald head. The other boys smirked, either at my boldness or my feeble-mindedness.

"Go home now, Saul. Find your father and put this question to him."

I was young enough that I did exactly as instructed. I left the academy, detoured around the statue of Sandon that had so terrified me as a smaller child, and ran through the streets to the compound where I lived with my parents, my sisters, and a multitude of servants.

I found my father in the large, dusty store-room that was attached to our house. Father had many such store-rooms and warehouses, but this had been his first, and it was here that he liked to gather administrators from around his far-flung enterprises. From this nerve-center, great caravans forged overland past the forbidding eastward mountains, and fleets of ships sailed down the River Cydon into what the Romans called the Mare Nostrum, ranging even past Iberia into the Sea of Atlas.

Father looked up from some calculations he was making with a stick in the dirt floor. He gestured for his men to continue their discussion and walked quickly over to me. He was stocky and somewhat bowlegged, and he walked with a kind of swagger. He had a large head covered with thick, dark curls and a full beard. I would grow up to resemble him.

I repeated what I had asked Cleanthes. Father's face, always ready to smile, became serious.

"This is what the Jews believe," he said. "That their Holy One created and rules the entire world."

"Aren't we Jews?"

Father glanced toward his administrators, who were now arguing and waving their hands at one another.

"We are also Roman citizens, Saul. This is our greatest strength and our protection."

"But I am studying in the academy, Father. No one speaks of Jews or even Romans. Nearly every word is about Greeks. Long-dead Greeks."

At this Father laughed so loud and for so long that I was afraid he would make himself ill. He laughed until he coughed and then after a while his coughing wore itself down to a sputter. He reached out to tenderly caress my small head.

"My darling Saul," he said. "Here is the secret of life. When you are with the Jews, be a Jew. When you are with the Romans, be a Roman. And always, always, think like a Greek."

Father was less than an ardent member of the Jewish community, although he always donated for sacrifices in keeping with his wealth and position. Aramaic was spoken in our home rather than Hebrew. Most Jewish boys of my age would normally be sent to the synagogue for training in the law. My visions presented a problem; there was doubt that I would ever be approved for study. I knew that this was one of the reasons that Father had distanced himself. One day I overheard my parents discussing my prospects.

"Perhaps," Mother said hopefully, "the Holy One, Blessed be He, has set our son apart, and is calling him to some special task."

"What kind of god," Father said, "gives an innocent child such terrors and then neither takes them away nor provides any explanation or understanding? And what good are the pompous servants of such a god if they are also helpless? How will Saul inherit all that I have built here?"

My dreams left me often moody and exhausted; I frightened other children. I grew up, loved by my family, moderately successful in the academy, and without many friends. On a warm spring day in my seventeenth year, Father handed me a small bag of gold and directed me to an unremarkable temple near the river. Gathering my barely sufficient courage, I hesitated outside and then entered by the designated side door.

Burning incense filled the air. An older woman, respectfully and conservatively dressed, greeted me with an assessing glance. She accepted my offering without comment.

"You must be prepared," she said.

Two servants appeared and conducted me to a series of heated pools located in another room. When I was acceptably bathed, dried and anointed with oils, and wearing a short linen robe provided by the temple, they returned me to the first woman. She drew aside a curtain and gestured that I should pass through.

In the next room were three women, well-wrapped in rich fabrics. They were barefoot and with bare arms. Their hair was oiled and pulled back off their faces, their eyes painted in what was then called the Egyptian fashion.

One was dark, with features that spoke of Asia. She smiled coyly. The second woman was round-faced and plump. Her lips were set, as if she had eaten something unpleasant. The last woman had radiant eyes, translucent skin and a narrow face framed by thick black hair. She was probably ten or twelve years older than I. She took three quick steps and stood before me, grinning as if we were about to share a private joke.

"Come, she said. "It isn't awful, you'll see."

She held out her hand and I went with her to another room, where she primly dropped her robes and stood naked before me. I have never forgotten her eyes: they were like the green stones called *smaragdos* in Greek. My mother and sisters wore them in amulets and rings. Years later, I would learn that in Hebrew the stones were known as *bareket*, lightning flashes. They were among the twelve stones placed on the Hoşen, the breastplate worn by the high priest in the Jerusalem Temple.

The woman's body was painted with geometric markings, swirls and dots that highlighted her slender hips, small breasts and her shaven sex. She led me to a perfumed couch where she confused and amazed me, brought me to tears and then to great bouts of laughter. For a few brief yet eternal-seeming moments, it was as if I were experiencing one of my visions, though I was not afraid.

Afterward, the green-eyed woman said she was married, the mother of two small children. Our assignation was dedicated to her chosen goddess, the only time in her life she would break her marriage vows. I promised I would never forget her, and I never have. Afterward, on the dazed walk home, I realized that I hadn't asked her name.

When I told Cleanthes about the woman in the temple, he laughed heartily.

"This practice," he said, "is older than the Greeks, and even older than your Hebrews. Men have always wanted women, and so we have bought them, taken them or married them. But there is another tradition, from a time, they say, when all the gods were female. In this tradition, every free woman must one time in her life go to the temple and give herself to a stranger. "

"But my mother has never...."

Cleanthes composed his face into the flat scowl which he thought made him look like a serious scholar. But there was humor in his eyes.

"Your mother is a Hebrew," he said, "born and bound under the law of Moses. Your father, you may have noticed, indulges her in this, although your presence here in this academy – to say nothing of his sending you to the temple by the river -- shows that he has a wider way of looking at the world."

"What of my sisters?"

"Hebrews also. They will marry and likely assume the beliefs of their husbands, unless they have some of your questioning qualities. There is no real role today among your people for independent, powerful women."

"But why did my father...?"

"In the Greek tradition, there are woman who go with men at their choice and convenience, taking lovers as they will, studying, conversing openly, arguing and disagreeing. Strong women – they are known as *hierodules.* A Hebrew woman who behaved in such a way would, I believe, be called a *zonah* – a woman who can be bought for a price. But there is also the term *Qedesha* -- a priestess or consecrated woman. Such women served the gods that were worshiped in Canaan before the Hebrews came. Canaanites believed that their gods inhabited standing columns, or sacred groves. Your Holy One was particularly annoyed by these gods and also, presumably, by the priestesses who performed rites before them."

Cleanthes laughed again and clapped me on the shoulder.

"Welcome to manhood, young Saul. You have truly been caught up into the heavens! We call this *harpāzo*, and it is a rare moment, to be treasured all your life."

From then on, I admit, I occasionally visited the whores of Tarsus, and I went with women after I came to Jerusalem. I fell in love several times — or so I thought. I discovered and rediscovered the bittersweet pain of uncertainty, and I grew familiar with concupiscence, courtship and release. But in all those early years I never again approached the wonderment and awe that were granted me by a noble virtuous woman in a riverside Tarsan temple.

My visions grew ever more powerful; I became ever more paralyzed. It was a lonely state for a developing mind. I had no star to chart my life's course upon, nor any fellow-travelers with whom I could commiserate about the hardships of the journey. I began to believe that eventually I would be swallowed up and never return.

When I turned seventeen, synagogue officials came and told my father that "the Greek influence" must have exacerbated dangerous in-born tendencies in me. It was written in the Tanakh, they said, that *daimons* were evil influences, perhaps even false gods sent to lead men astray. Increased donations for sacrifice might be beneficial. Failing that, I should be taken to the synagogue, and there subjected to physical hardships: starvation, immersion in water, the whip. Father listened politely, without question or comment. Then he had the officials summarily removed from our home. Despite our family's long cultural history, that was the end of our association with Jewish life in Tarsus.

My academy studies intensified. Cleanthes and other teachers taught me that the Greeks believed *daimons* to be intermediaries between men and gods. They could be good as well as evil. Some had even thought of their own *daimons* as a kind of higher personal authority – either giving advice or – when no good course of action was apparent – remaining silent. We engaged in long discussions about whether these *daimons* were corporeal, with independent existence, or were merely products of our own minds.

Cleanthes tried to teach me to inhabit my visions, to abide in them. He thought this might either give me power over them or cause them to fade away like smoke. Once, when I related to him a dream in which I had been pursued underwater and eaten by a gigantic sea-monster, Cleanthes reminded me how Perseus saved Andromeda by slaying the sea-beast named Cetus. We both laughed. The summer before I had almost drowned when I slipped into the River Cydnus while chasing fish. I was no Perseus. And I was then, as now, of insignificant stature and limited physical strength.

Did I hear a voice, Cleanthes asked, or voices? Was I ordered to think or do evil? Was I confronted by disturbing images such as natural catastrophes or war? Could I be experiencing a series of divinations? The work was hard and the more I chased after my visions the further they seemed to recede. Weeks and then months went by without any unusual experiences, an interim of relative peace. Eventually Cleanthes said that it was long past time for me to live the life that had been prepared for me.

Father tried to launch me into the world of commerce, but as soon as I tried to reach beyond the safety of academy, home and family, I was overcome by the most powerful visions I had ever had. I was incapacitated for ten days, lying in my bed, delirious to outside eyes, nursed by Mother and diligent servants. I do not remember what I experienced. When I came back to myself -- an emaciated shell – Father took me aside and said he had made a decision.

"I do not want to lose you, my son," he said. Tears ran down his dear face. "But I see that I am losing you anyway. I have heard of a man in Jerusalem, a great Rebhi, a Pharisee. He is said to be an expert in *merkabah,* visions such as you have experienced. Perhaps he can help you."

I wept beside him. I did not want to leave Tarsus, my family, my home. But I also knew that I could not survive as I was. And so, within a few days, accompanied by four armed servants and an ass loaded with jewels, clothing -- and a fat bag of gold -- I set off for Jerusalem. In a fold of my robe, I carried a last gift, pressed into my hand by my weeping mother, whom I would never see again. It was a small unpolished *bareket*: to keep me safe, she said, and to remind me of home. Mother could not have known that the stone also called up tender memories of my riverside lover. I have it still.

JERUSALEM, ROMAN JUDAEA [28-37 CE]

Jerusalem – and Judaism -- inflamed me, despite my longing for home and my resistance to anything Hebrew. I was a polyglot, unique but not special. Roman citizen, half-educated Hellenist, nominal Jew, son of a wealthy father. I had been raised to see a necessary and even pleasing unity in the world, and the naked fury of the Jewish Holy One was like a blast from a fiery furnace.

Gamaliel was the Rabbani, Jerusalem's greatest teacher, grandson of Rebhi Hillel. He was a man of middle age, thick of body, bent from decades of study. His beard was full and gray, with a smattering of white hairs. Gamaliel understood the Hebrew laws not simply as axioms to be blindly followed, but as starting points for the exercise of his magnificent mind. Others would come to him with questions; he would first tease out their unspoken intent and then carry them along with him on mind journeys that left them – and everyone present – on the shores of worlds never before conceived or imagined.

I was a dutiful son, and still hopeful that my visions might be dispelled through study. I decided to apply myself diligently to the practical logic of the Pharisees. I can confess today that I never succeeded. I hear the Hebrew laws in my mind first in Greek and only then can I slowly, incompletely re-translate into the language of the Jews. Among his many scrolls, Gamaliel had a crumbling Greek Torah. According to legend, it had been translated from the Hebrew by seventy Alexandrian rebhis. This moldy, fragile compilation became the locus of my study. Rebhi Gamaliel gently but firmly drew me out and I began to discover opinions I never knew I had.

Each morning, Rebhi Gamaliel would read from the law and then question me on my understanding. This was almost perfunctory – I quickly intuited that he did not intend to make me into a scholar, or even into a traditional literate upper-class Jew, one who might someday aspire to leadership in the community. Once we had exhausted my pathetic attempts at Hebrew, Rebhi Gamaliel would bring out one or more of his Greek scrolls -- philosophers, poets and playwrights from ancient times. He knew I had had a reasonable – although incomplete -- exposure to these works and he seemed sincerely interested in my opinions of their meaning and applicability to our present lives. We switched languages from Hebrew to Aramaic, in which I was more fluent.

Rebhi Gamaliel was surprisingly conversant with the philosophical traditions I had learned in Tarsus. He applied this knowledge in ongoing debate, but in the end, he could not make me comprehend why the supposed creator of the universe, despite immense and unlimited power, took an almost human interest in the affairs of men – and especially in the destiny of a small arrogant group of undeserving desert people living in the backwaters of civilization.

Rebhi Gamaliel listened with a gentle smile to my espousals of atomism, of *physis* and *logos*, of the immanence and transcendence of the god-concept propounded my Tarsan teachers.

"I have chosen to believe in a personal God," he said one morning in his study. "I do not need stories of the Red Sea parting, or the waters rising to destroy all but Noah and his family. Like your first teachers, I seek truth in the way human minds can interpret given laws. Truth emerges in the dialogue between men of different minds and training."

I worked hard, but I still found time for fine food, drink and as always, women. I have sometimes quaked with shame at my dissolute younger life, but I can also recognize that I was seeking the brief epiphany provided by my first experience back in Tarsus.

Rebhi Gamaliel was indulgent of my worldly excesses. He had more than one wife, concubines as befit a man of his high station, and many children. I envied him and occasionally fantasized that I might follow him into Pharasaic leadership.

During my third, and final year, Gamaliel taught me the four levels of truth according to the Pharisees. Of these the most important, he said, was *sod,* the most hidden meaning. I recognized this idea from my earlier studies – and from Gamaliel's Greek Torah, as *mysteria,* the secret teachings.

Jerusalem at that time was a cauldron – no, a cesspool – of divergent Jewish factions. The Sanhedrin, the ruling council for Jerusalem Jews, was composed of two primary factions. Sadducees, priests of the Temple, held direct lines of control from the Roman overlords. It was they who collected tribute and taxes, and who also profited from the costs of Temple sacrifice and ritual. They tended to see any revival of the Jewish notion of primacy as dangerous to their position. They knew that they had the most to lose from revolution or rebellion and so tried to maintain a somnolent population. The Romans, masters at governing diverse and resistive subjugated peoples, had determined long ago that the greedy, self-interested Sadducees would best serve to control the fractious Jerusalem Jews.

Pharisees were teachers of the people, community leaders who held meetings for prayer and discussion in their homes. Most had professions of their own; only a few Pharisees lived like Gamaliel as philosophers and teachers, earning their living from community contributions and tuition from rich students. Pharisees continually tried to explain civil events – to themselves and to the people – in terms of Jewish history and the law. Some Pharisees emphasized the prophetic books, going so far as to endorse the messianic threads that had always formed a strong component of Jewish thought. Others, like Gamaliel, cautioned patience and acceptance, choosing to see Roman rule as yet another test set by the Holy One.

In addition to these differences, Sadducees and Pharisees were split on a major doctrinal point: Sadducees did not believe there was any life after the death of the body, while for Pharisees an individual could merit eternal rest in *Pardes,* where the Holy One dwells.

There were also any number of radical groups: Zealots, revolutionaries, and followers of different so-called messiahs living and dead. Each of these small claques, forming and dissipating on what seemed to be a daily basis, hated the others more than any of them hated Rome. Each also claimed to possess the true message of the Holy One.

It was while I was living with Rebhi Gamaliel that I heard of Yeshua, the teacher from Galilee. At first I thought he was just another of the many local saviors who came and went, rose and fell – often sacrificed to the sword or the cross. There were also many itinerant mages and sorcerers who enjoyed different degrees of notoriety. These were more tolerated by the Sadducees and the Romans than were the messiahs, because they were entertainers who tended to divert the people from any ideas of rebellion.

This Yeshua, however, was developing a different kind of reputation among the people. For one, he was not a rebel. He did not advocate overthrow of the Roman hegemony. He was also a healer. He had famously cast out what were called devils from men and women. Some said that he had raised the dead. He drifted around the area north of Jerusalem with a group of his kin, fellow peasants who had been carpenters, masons or fishermen. It was said that Yeshua could perfectly recite and reference all the law and the prophets. He was supported by an informal cohort of upper-class women -- relatives of high officials and merchants, and even, according to rumor, a proconsul's wife. He never thought of food, drink or shelter – these were provided, both for his men and for the multitudes who more and more were clamoring to be near him.

I also heard condemnatory stories about Yeshua: he was really a Zealot; he called himself King of the Jews; he was nothing more than a wizard. I decided to find out for myself, but first I spoke to my master, Rebhi Gamaliel.

I found him in his study, immersed as usual in his scholarly work. He looked up and it took a moment for his eyes to focus on me.

"Have you heard, Rabban, of the man called Yeshua?"

Gamaliel sighed deeply.

"A unique individual," he said. "He turns the law on its head, speaks of a new covenant between the Holy One, Blessed be He, and the people. And he's a crowd pleaser, too. He uses magic to underscore his message."

"I would like to go see him."

"What would be your intent?"

"I am always interested in new ideas…"

Gamaliel smiled.

"Sometimes to a fault, Saul. I think it was the Roman Cicero who spoke out against rashness, and the need for careful application of logic."

I smiled back. This was a familiar issue between us.

"This man seems to be something not seen before," I said.

"Then go, observe, and give me your impressions when you return."

The Greeks wrote that all love begins with an appreciation of individual beauty -- and that love of beauty is first found in Eros. I wanted this to be true, but my youthful couplings – with the one exception -- were only poor imitations of love. My first teachers believed that most men and women never find love beyond such animal rutting. Only a few, they said, manage adoration. This pulls them beyond themselves into a helpless love of beauty – of man or woman, of the unspoiled innocence of childhood. Fewer still are then surprised into love of all creation.

I was immune to the words of philosophers on this topic until the day I went to hear the man Yeshua, on a hill above the Sea of Galilee. I stood off to one side, as I would later at his crucifixion. A moist breeze drifted up from the water, although it did not cool the ardor of the multitude that strained to hear Yeshua's every word. Several women stood at a distance. All were courtly and dignified, wearing fine garments that would not have been out of place in my sisters' overflowing wardrobes. One woman, flanked by a contingent of armed retainers, held herself aloof. A few strands of reddish hair escaped her cloak and fluttered wildly in the wind. She felt me staring and returned my gaze. Under the force of her dark eyes, I was an insect pinned to a table; for a moment, I forgot about Yeshua. Although the woman appeared to be about my own age, there was something timeless about her, as if she embodied the living soul of the *kosmos*. She looked away and I found that I had been holding my breath.

Afterward, I watched the people approach Yeshua, hesitant and almost fearful. Some had questions. Others just wanted to stand in his presence, as if they could clutch a bit longer at what they imagined he had offered them.

He was in conversation with an intense, muscular man whom I would later know as Cephas. Yeshua's eyes found mine and he gestured for me to come forward. Cephas put a proprietary hand on his shoulder, but Yeshua shook himself loose. He gestured to me again.

I was very conscious of my appearance. I was wrapped in the finest linen, draped with jewelry more suitable for dinner at my father's home – or a king's palace -- than a dusty hillside in the Galilee.

Yeshua's face was untroubled. He was impervious, I thought at the time, to challenge or harm. His eyes were cold and clear, honey-colored, like the mythical *lyngurium* described by Theophrastus.

"Rebhi," I began, and then had no more words.

"What is it that you wish, my friend?"

"Rebhi…."

Cephas stood two paces away, watching us carefully.

"How can a person follow you?"

Cephas snorted and strode away. Yeshua followed him with his eyes for a moment, then he turned back to me, his gaze taking in my clothes, my jewels, my luxurious sandals. He sniffed at the perfume I had put on before setting out.

"Put away all these things," he said. He reached out a hand, a gesture that included all that I wore, all that I was.

"Put away all these things," he said again. "Leave your studies, your knowledge, your teachers. Leave your home, your family, your wealth. Follow your heart."

Yeshua stared into my soul for what seemed like an eternity. And then, when he recognized me for who I was -- who I could be at that time and place -- he dimmed his light.

"Go," he said softly. "Return when you are ready."

Yeshua turned easily and walked off toward the small knot of people, his people, who were waiting and watching our brief interchange. All centered their attention on him as he came close, as if he was their truth, their food and drink. The young woman was nowhere to be seen.

After returning from Galilee, I was lost. My prior studies with Gamaliel meant nothing. Why learn about rules, judgments and fear? I was besotted with Yeshua's calm certainty, and the piercing glare of the young woman with blue eyes.

I had not even spoken to her. He had asked me to follow him and I hadn't. Why not? This was the question that plagued me, as I sat before Gamaliel day after day, trying to comprehend the law.

Rebhi Gamaliel called me one morning to a private interview. I thought we would be discussing a specific argument from the laws or the prophets, for it was the way of Gamaliel – as all great teachers – to work from analogy.

But Gamaliel wanted to talk about Yeshua.

"Does he call himself our Messiah, Saul? Some say that he does."

I was taken aback and could not answer immediately. This was the great Rebhi Gamaliel, Jerusalem's most respected scholar, asking the opinion of a callow youth – for that was what I knew myself to be. And I could not remember much of what Yeshua had said, something about love.

"He is a rough, square man, Rabban, perhaps thirty years of age. A peasant from near the Galilee. His movements are those of a man who knows hard work. His voice is powerful but soft, like a perfumed breeze. He can bring tears to the most resistive listener."

If Gamaliel thought I was withholding something, he gave no sign. He nodded and we began our usual studies. But a growing conviction that I had missed a precious opportunity in Galilee made me a poorer student day by day.

Rebhi Gamaliel rose to pray each morning well before dawn. Then he left his house without breaking his fast, and walked robustly through the streets of Jerusalem until it was time for a small mid-morning meal. Afterward, I would go into his study, where I would find him studying one or another selection from the untamed wilderness of scrolls that covered every horizontal surface.

Each day, just before we ended our discussion, Rebhi Gamaliel would ask me if I had had any new visions. Looking back, I can see that this was his chief interest all along. My father's commission to Gamaliel – and the heavy bag of gold that paid for my years in his home – had been intended to either clarify or excise the apparitions that prevented me from returning home.

We often discussed my ongoing dreams of rising into the air. One afternoon I described an especially vivid night-dream.

"I was in a chariot," I said, "carried by some kinds of beasts..."

Gamaliel's expression became so intense that I feared I must have been overtaken by an evil spirit. He stared into my eyes.

"With many faces?"

I became more confused.

"Yes... yes, Rabban. But they were unclear, as if they were melting into one another. I rose up out of the city..."

"What city?"

"Why... Jerusalem. This city. I could see the mountains, and the Sea of Galilee, and the Mare Nostrum to the east. I looked down at the Temple and all the people doing business there."

"Did you see anything in the sky?"

"In the sky?"

"Yes, in the clouds."

"It was a dream, Rabban, and it is mostly gone now."

Rebhi Gamaliel rose and hurriedly searched among his scrolls. He came back and read to me in Hebrew, slowly so that he could be certain I would understand.

"I looked, and I saw a windstorm coming out of the north—an immense cloud with flashing lightning and surrounded by brilliant light. The center of the fire looked like glowing metal, and in the fire was what looked like four living creatures. In appearance their form was human, but each of them had four faces and four wings. Their legs were straight; their feet were like those of a calf and gleamed like burnished bronze. Under their wings on their four sides they had human hands. All four of them had faces and wings, and the wings of one touched the wings of another. Each one went straight ahead; they did not turn as they moved.

"Their faces looked like this: Each of the four had the face of a human being, and on the right side each had the face of a lion, and on the left the face of an ox; each also

had the face of an eagle. Such were their faces. They each had two wings spreading out upward, each wing touching that of the creature on either side; and each had two other wings covering its body. Each one went straight ahead. Wherever the spirit would go, they would go, without turning as they went. The appearance of the living creatures was like burning coals of fire or like torches. Fire moved back and forth among the creatures; it was bright, and lightning flashed out of it. The creatures sped back and forth like flashes of lightning.

"As I looked at the living creatures, I saw a wheel on the ground beside each creature with its four faces. This was the appearance and structure of the wheels: They sparkled like topaz, and all four looked alike. Each appeared to be made like a wheel intersecting a wheel. As they moved, they would go in any one of the four directions the creatures faced; the wheels did not change direction as the creatures went. Their rims were high and awesome, and all four rims were full of eyes all around."

Gamaliel closed his eyes, his lips moving soundlessly.

"Yes," I said, "yes. That is very much like what I saw. I remember now, is this not from the prophet Ezekiel? What does this mean, Rabban?"

Gamaliel opened his eyes and stared at me. He shook his head decisively.

"That will be all for today, Saul. Go now, and walk the city until it is time for dinner. I have invited guests."

Young men are fools, as I have said, and are easily led by their emotions. I had by then studied with Rebhi Gamaliel for nearly three full years: it pains me to say that I judged his gentle wisdom, his compassion and patience, as weaknesses. I saw things in the absolute – something was either all right or all wrong. For Rebhi Gamaliel there was always an exception, a different way of turning a question so that it exposed a new possibility. I had no patience for such subtlety. I wanted answers, resolutions. I knew that my vision was important – both for me, and perhaps also for him -- and I was more than disappointed that he did not trust me enough to impart any meaning or context. But it was not my place to demand an explanation from the great Rabban, and so I stalked petulantly through the city until it was time to come in for dinner.

Rebhi Gamaliel loved to extoll the virtues of simplicity in all things. His home, though large and well-furnished, exemplified this philosophy. I was used to a finer display; my father often teased my mother by saying that if she should ever leave Tarsus, all the city's potters, furniture makers, weavers and metalsmiths would starve within days.

I was also used to lively conversation during meals: my sisters and my mother chattering about things they had seen in the city -- their latest purchases, adventures and scandals involving friends or extended family. My father, when he was not overseeing one of his many holdings, would sit aloof in his throne-like chair at the head of the table. Although he seemed to notice everything, he rarely made comments. From time to time, business associates and their families might come for gatherings where wine and after-dinner philosophizing – *symposion* -- could flow quite freely.

This Greek practice was acceptable to Jerusalem's Pharisees, so long as the meal was preceded by an appropriate *berakhah*. At my father's table, this blessing had instead taken the form of a *libation,* wine spilled out in honor of one god or another. It was never specified whether the sacrifice was in honor of the Jewish Holy One, or some local deity. I remember being pleased when I was old enough to have the wine cup passed to me, indicating that I could speak and expect to be heard. Later, when I was living as a prisoner in Rome, my friend Lucius Annaeus Seneca taught me that this practice derived from the time of Plato, although he used the Latin word *convivium.*

At Rebhi Gamaliel's table, Pharisees, Sadducees, Gentiles, Romans, Samaritans and foreigners of every nation might appear. Meals consisted of hard-crusted bread, fresh fruits and vegetables, small amounts of lamb or chicken, water and dark wine. Everything was served in plain wooden bowls and unglazed crockery jars.

The first guests that night were known to me. Nicodemus and Joseph were wealthy merchants. They were also leaders of the Sanhedrin. Nicodemus was short, olive-skinned and stocky. He had a black beard, deep-set dark eyes and a prominent beaked nose that appeared to have been broken more than once. Despite his fine clothes and obvious learning, he had the gnarled hands of a stone-cutter. He spoke in short, declarative sentences, making his points quickly and then sitting in silence as if daring anyone to contradict him. Joseph was an extremely tall man who always wore bright-colored robes. He moved easily and with power, though he was no longer young. He was light-skinned and his spectral eyes glowed like pearls from the Red Sea. His flowing hair and beard were the color of well-worn silver. Joseph was sometimes called Scythianus because of his striking appearance and his lifetime of travel in the east. He framed his words effortlessly, his voice lifting and falling almost as if he were reciting a poem. I thought that he enjoyed speaking, enjoyed the effect he had on others.

We were just going to the table when four additional guests arrived, three women and a man. Maryam and Martha were sisters, accompanied by their brother Lazarus. They lived in the town of Bethany, just outside Jerusalem. I knew them from previous appearances at dinner. Maryam and Martha were young Jewish women of marrying age, adventurous in speech and tone, unbetrothed as far as I knew. They always flirted discreetly with me, as if I was a distant cousin. Lazarus was probably two or three years younger than I. He was a handsome boy, bursting with health. But they were all rendered invisible for me by the third woman. She was also Maryam, introduced with smiles all around as Maryam Magdala. I thought this meant that she was from a town called Magdala, but Rebhi Gamaliel later explained to me that this was a local Aramaic idiom meaning "tower" or "watchtower." Maryam Magdala, he said, was a Nabataean princess, first cousin to Aretas Philopatras, the new ruler of Damascus. Her home was far to the south, in the city of Rekem, in Arabia. She was the young woman from Yeshua's sermon on the mount.

When Maryam Magdala shrugged off her rich cloak, her unruly red hair sprang free -- long, lustrous and lying sinuously along her neck. It had rained all day, and Maryam's hair crinkled at the ends, causing me to think of Egypt or even far-off Nubia. She had a high forehead, a square jawline, and a long and pleasantly tapered nose. Close up, her almond-shaped eyes were the same deep blue as the jewels called *sapir* in Hebrew, or *sappheiros* in Greek. Light seemed to gather in those wide-set eyes, ready to burst forth at any moment. I thought I saw flecks of gold and a trace of royal purple in the blue -- and then I shyly looked away. Maryam was well-dressed in Roman style: she wore a red linen *stola* under a bright green silk *pallas*, clasped at her breast with a golden brooch. My immature mind immediately wondered why it would have been necessary for me to give up my wealth in order to follow Yeshua, while Maryam Magdala obviously maintained an opulent lifestyle. In my old age, pondering this question, I have thought: perhaps it was Yeshua who followed her.

Men – and boys – are visual beings. Beauty can halt us in our tracks and bind our tongues. We also tend to believe – to our frequent disappointment – that the beautiful and the good go hand in hand. In Maryam Magdala these two qualities truly met and were blended with a prodigious intelligence. I believe that I pledged my life to her -- as only a smitten boy can do -- on that very night. And of course, I could not know then that we would become comrades and friends in the years to come.

I was astonished at how calmly Maryam shared her opinions, and also at how the others listened to her. In subsequent days, when I sat in Gamaliel's house, puzzling over the law, I would recall a fold of her robe, the extension of her hand as she reinforced an argument. I would meditate on her wide brow, her high cheekbones and her rich full lips. The lower lip was thicker than its companion above, and was often pursed in what could have been sadness or regret if not for the wild brilliance at play in her eyes.

Years later, when we met again in Arabia, it was both the same and also entirely different. Maryam became a person to me as well as a goddess. She breathed, moved. I could sit nearby and smell her, study the small pores of her skin, the way her upper lip retracted when she was thinking hard, revealing the tips of her white teeth. I could minutely – if cautiously – memorize the encrusted desert dirt on her toes, the callouses on the pads of her feet. And her hands, toughened but still somehow delicate, her narrower than expected wrists, the small crescent scar on the inside of her right fore-arm, sometimes exposed from beneath her robe. I thought I could tell when she was menstruating: her eyes were deeper in their sockets, her gaze was less direct and her speech was quicker and more succinct. She smelled differently, metallic – or this was all in my fired puerile imagination.

I did not offer much to the conversation that evening. I remember that someone, I think it was Joseph, mentioned Yohannon the Baptizer, recently killed by Herod.

"He was neither Pharisee nor Saduccee, Zealot or Essene," Martha said. "To the people in the towns and villages, he seemed like a prophet from times long past, rough-dressed, his hair and beard uncut and unkempt. He refused to eat meat. Living, it was said on honey and roots. "

"I have heard that he dressed in the skins of wild animals," said Lazarus.

"He wore the same rough cloth as all the other peasants," Martha said, with a sisterly smirk.

"Yohannon attracted many," Joseph said, "especially among the young men who had been employed in the rebuilding of Sapphoris. Herod took notice when he began baptizing his followers in the Jordan River. The crowds grew in size. Herod, always cautious, feared rebellion and so he had Yohannon arrested and eventually executed."

"And what of Yeshua? "Rebhi Gamaliel said. "He speaks to many in the Galilee."

I felt Maryam Magdala's eyes on me.

"Yeshua is a younger cousin of the Baptizer," Joseph said. "During Yohannon's ministry, Yeshua was apparently content to take a lesser place, although he was locally known both as a healer and for his mastery of the laws."

Nicodemus shoved his elbows forward on the table. His forearms were corded with muscle; his veins were thick and prominent.

"After Yohannon was killed," he said, "some of the young men coalesced around Yeshua. Although Yeshua didn't baptize, his message soon attracted large crowds."

Maryam Magdala tucked a strand of her thick mane behind a small, well-shaped ear.

"Some months ago," she said, "I went to hear him in the hills around Nazareth. He seemed in complete control of his teaching, as if every word, its placement and intonation, carried deeper meaning than could immediately be perceived."

"They say he is also a healer," Rebhi Gamaliel said. "Even as you are, Maryam."

"I was ill," Lazarus said, shaking his head slowly. "I became weak, could not hold down food. Oils and unguents were tried, to no avail. Then Yeshua came. He simply spoke with me, and I began to be better."

I lowered my eyes and was silent. Gamaliel knew that I had seen Yeshua, and also knew that I had been unable to leave everything and follow him. Maryam Magdala, with what I would later learn was her usual perspicacity, leaned toward me and touched my arm. I could feel heat from the pads of her fingers.

"What is it, Saul?"

I hesitated, and the pressure of Maryam's fingers increased. I looked up and met her eyes.

"I went to see him," I said. "When he spoke on the hill overlooking the Galilee. I failed him. He said that to follow him is to forsake all else."

Maryam smiled then, a boundlessly kind smile that reminded me of my sisters.

"You have not failed him yet, Saul," she said. "Perhaps there will be other opportunities."

I remained mute, the question in my heart unasked: do you remember me at all?

"Some call him a zealot," Nicodemus said. "A dangerous man, who might yet cause a great deal of trouble."

"He does stir up the people when he talks of the coming Kingdom," Joseph said. "But he doesn't take them so far that they become uncontrolled."

"It's true," Martha said. "He is masterful. We all leave him feeling elated but not angry. Hopeful, yet in a peaceful way. He speaks of love."

Lazarus looked around the table.

"But Yeshua also said, did he not, 'Whoever finds his life will lose it, and whoever loses his life for my sake will find it.'"

I was still with Gamaliel when Yeshua rode triumphantly into Jerusalem, when the people cheered him and it briefly seemed as if he would lead a rebellion. Then he was taken, judged and crucified.

Several women, and one boy, whom I later knew as Yohannon, Yeshua's cousin, stood witness. Maryam Magdala was among them, again surrounded by her armed retinue. None of Yeshua's male followers were anywhere to be seen. The Roman soldiers, bored with their jobs, moved slowly through the field of crosses.

I watched Yeshua suffer terribly, as all of them do. He didn't cry out when they drove the nails, though his blood ran thickly into the ground. I looked up and the sky was crimson; I thought I heard the baying of hounds. There were so many crosses, so many men nailed to them. Some were already dead, some gasped out their last agonized breaths. Crows came by the hundreds to feast on the choicest morsels.

I have heard that a crucified man can live for two or even three days on a cross. Some families bribed the Roman soldiers to break the crucified one's legs; death came from suffocation soon after. But that was not to be the case for Yeshua. A Roman soldier approached and gave him something to drink from a moistened rag at the end of a stick. Yeshua sucked gratefully on the rag and then his eyes flew open. He tried to speak, failed and released one last phlegmatic breath. Another soldier pricked his side with a spear; blood began to flow. We all waited, each of us thinking our own thoughts, but he did not seem to breathe again. It was near sundown. The Passover was about to begin.

Then Joseph and Nicodemus appeared. They were richly dressed, and they walked like men who were used to giving orders. They were accompanied by two servants. Joseph gestured at the soldiers. They approached arrogantly, as soldiers will. When they drew near to Joseph their demeanor changed. They bowed deeply. Joseph pointed toward Yeshua hanging above them. He said something and the soldiers without hesitation began to lower Yeshua to the ground. The women came closer, watching as the servants pulled the nails out of the cross. A linen sheet was laid on the ground next to Yeshua's body and the two servants gently lifted him and lay him in it. They wound the sheet around him, lifted him again, and together they and Joseph and Nicodemus took him away. The small group of women, wailing in despair, and the boy Yohannon, followed. Discreetly, I followed as well.

Not all the women wailed. Maryam Magdala walked rigid and silent, flanked by her guardians. Her red hair was barely restrained by her cloak, her head was unbowed, and her eyes were as unreadable as the roiling sea. She was trembling, but I thought she shook with rage rather than grief. The small procession, with me at a distance, followed a path into an area of great estates. Joseph and Nicodemus went through a small gate in a high stone wall. Maryam followed, and the others lingered just outside. I found out later that this was Joseph's own villa, and this was his magnificent garden, with its tall trees, luxurious plantings and carefully trimmed vines.

I watched as Joseph, Nicodemus and the manservants carried Yeshua into the villa. At the door, Joseph turned to Maryam. She held a small alabaster jar in her hands; I hadn't noticed it until then. Maryam followed Joseph inside, her attendants took up positions by the door, and then there was nothing in the gathering twilight but the sounds of those who remained at the gate.

Let me say it now: the Temple curtain was not torn in two when Yeshua died. The earth did not shake and rocks did not split, although that is what the Christ-followers say. Who among the living actually remembers? It was almost eighty years ago; even the Temple itself is no more, torn stone from stone by Titus' Legions.

Maryam Magdala and the others never came to Gamaliel's again. After Yeshua's crucifixion, I was restless and began neglecting my studies even more than I had previously. I was rootless, angry, and impatient with Gamaliel's belief in a middle course. I gradually fell in with a cadre of like-minded young men. Without wisdom to guide us, we saw power as something to be sought above all things. And for Jews in Jerusalem, the only power, such as it was, resided in either the Sanhedrin or with the Temple priesthood.

When Yeshua was under suspicion, it was the Sadducees who clamored for his destruction. Some of his followers, they knew, wanted to believe that he was a new Messiah come to rid Judaea of the Romans. He was therefore a threat to their power and must be neutralized, in a manner that would ideally make the people fearful of rising up in any way against the established order.

After Yeshua disappeared, there was frequent debate in the Sanhedrin about the remnant of his followers, now calling themselves Nazarenes. Led by Cephas and Yaakov, Yeshua's brother, the Nazarenes themselves were composed of several factions. Some favored armed insurrection against Rome. Others were developing a theology centered in Yeshua's eventual otherworldly return.

I found Rebhi Gamaliel seated, as usual, in his study. His work table was covered in scrolls, some very rare and valuable. He was looking at a high point in the wall, though I knew he was not seeing anything beyond the caverns of his rarefied mind.

"Rabban," I asked, "Do you think Yeshua was the Messiah?"

Rebhi Gamaliel brought his gaze down and met my eyes.

"It doesn't matter what I think. If he is the Messiah, he will soon come back in glory and the world will change. Any resistance from men would be useless. If he is not, then he won't come and his movement will disappear like so many others."

He smiled sadly.

"How many Messiahs have I myself known in my fifty-five years? How many have died fighting the Romans? How many were stoned, burned or crucified?"

"People are saying that Yeshua rose from the dead."

Gamaliel shook himself.

"Let me posit a question, Saul. What if his body was taken by his followers, just so that they might keep people's interest alive even when their leader was dead?"

"But who...?"

"It could have been anyone. Yeshua was a touchstone for many people of many different viewpoints."

Rebhi Gamaliel focused his dark, small eyes on me. He was silent for a time. I waited. When he finally spoke, his face was bleak.

"It is difficult to know how to be a Jew these days, Saul. Some are Pharisees who teach the people the ways of the Law and who believe that understanding and following the Law are all that is important. Some are priests, Sadducees, who think that by adhering to the Temple rituals of sacrifice and purification they are the true and only Jews."

"But…"

He silenced me with a glance.

"And then there are those with narrower definitions, who define themselves in reaction to our Roman masters. To them, any earthly intermediary between the Holy One, Blessed Be He, and His chosen people is unacceptable. There are as many ways to resist in His name as there are grains of sand in the desert. Can you think of times in our history that this question was discussed?"

It was an easy question.

"The desert prophets refused the idea of kingship," I said. "To some of them, David and subsequent kings unjustly accrued the Holy One's power to themselves."

"Just so. We have a long tradition of resisting earthly authority in the name of the Holy One, blessed be He. Any man can name himself a new prophet – or Messiah – and if he is a sorcerer, or seems to know the law, and has a commanding voice, what better way to perfect his movement than for him to die and for his followers to begin a legend about his defeating death?"

"Do you see this remnant as a danger to our people?"

"I did not say that. Our people are in danger anyway. Rome has been consistent for centuries. She will work patiently to absorb or co-opt the leaders and traditions of those she conquers. But though she is a patient mistress, she is not soft. On the contrary, she is as capable of total destruction as the Tanakh says our ancestors were when they first came to this land."

"What if the people begin to believe the stories of Yeshua? What if they rise against the Romans, in larger numbers than they have before?"

"Then, my dear Saul, if Yeshua was not the Messiah, we are all doomed."

That very night I repeated my conversation with Rebhi Gamaliel to my friends. One of them was a nephew of the new High Priest, Jonathan Ananias.

"There is one of the Yeshua group," he said, "named Stephen. Not the highest leader, but the one who works hardest to excite the people. If he is successful, many lives, maybe all our lives, are at stake."

And so he took us to the High Priest. Soldiers were sent to detain Stephen, and he was brought before the Sanhedrin.

I sat at a distance as Stephen was questioned. Gamaliel, in his place of honor, was uncharacteristically uninvolved in the process. Stephen was accused of speaking against Moses and the Law, and of saying that Yeshua was the Messiah who had come to change the law.

Stephen began his defense by speaking calmly, but then he suddenly turned on the assembly and cursed them, and also all Jews:

"How stubborn you are, heathen still at heart and deaf to the truth. You always fight against the Holy Spirit. Like fathers, like sons. Was there ever a prophet whom your fathers did not persecute? They killed those who foretold the coming of the Righteous One; and now you have betrayed Him and murdered Him, you who received the Law as His angels gave it to you, and yet have not kept it."

Voices called out for Stephen's death, for violating the protocols of the Sanhedrin. I looked toward Rebhi Gamaliel and found that he was watching me. I turned away.

Stephen continued speaking amidst the uproar. He pointed toward the sky.

"Look, I see heaven open and the Son of Man standing at the right hand of the Holy One, Blessed be He."

At this the men in the room, Sadducees and Pharisees alike, rushed forward and dragged Stephen out to be stoned. I started to follow, but then looked back at the leaders of the Sanhedrin. They seemed suddenly like a group of beaten old men. I went out and watched as Stephen was killed.

After that I was not long with Gamaliel. One morning he called me to him.

"Your heart is not in your studies, Saul."

"I am fine, Rabban."

He shook his head sadly.

"I do not think so. Learning requires a cool head. Your brow burns with an unquenchable fever."

Soon afterward I left Gamaliel's house. I fell right in with friends who were agents of the High Priest. We told ourselves that we must rid Jerusalem of all those whose foolishness threatened the safety of the people.

I lived after that as a persecutor of Yeshua's followers, until I encountered him in spiritual form a few years later.

THE DAMASCUS ROAD [36 CE]

I have been told that blind men can see in their dreams. What I saw behind blinded eyes has never left me, has branded me and defined my life.

We were on horseback, on the Damascus road. We rode in haste, young men enflamed with the hunt, ready to throttle this false cult of the risen Yeshua before it could further spread its corruption.

We had no official status, but the High Priest had charged us solemnly: seek out these radicals, identify them, uncover their plans. Kill them if you can.

At a crossroads, my horse reared. I tried to keep my seat, fell backward and then I was engulfed in light. Faraway thunder echoed in from the sea. I was a pinpoint in a billowy world, whiteness ever deepening, rolled in a powerful current. I could have been underwater, yet I breathed.

They told me later that I lay as if dead: limbs stiff, eyes open but unseeing, my mouth stretched in silent agony.

I was lost to my own body, lost to the ground and to my companions, who must have been asking anxious questions, turning me here and there, searching for answers,

Slowly a figure took form. It was Yeshua, the crucified one. He bore the marks of his execution, scars on his hands and feet, and a longer scar along his side where the Roman soldier had speared him. His hair was lighter than I remembered, although it may just have been the brightness. His lips did not move but I heard his voice in the light: "Saul, Saul, why do you persecute me?" And then there was darkness.

I was three days in Damascus, in the house of Ananias the healer. It is all mixed up, so many years later. What was magic and what memory. The image that unhorsed me, Yeshua bathed in light, and then his face, unguarded and serene as it had been when I came to him in supplication above the Sea of Galilee.

When Ananias woke me, I was famished. He placed his hands on me and blessed me.

"You lay the whole time like stone," he said as my eyelids fluttered and his kindly face emerged from shadow. "We waited for you to die."

I did not speak, for I did not know what to say. My last thoughts before the flash of light had been about my mission, spying out Christ-followers in Damascus – Ananias would have been one of my targets.

Once Ananias was assured that I would live, he left me to sit alone in his small garden. I was told later that my eyes remained wide open, staring at things unseen. I never noticed the small fig tree, or the vines climbing the high back wall; I never touched the water brought by the gentle women of the house. I heard no sound of birdsong or human speech; there was only Yeshua's face, Yeshua's voice. It was as if we were sitting together, knees touching. I could see the lines etched into his face from his dying. I realized that he had a grandeur about him now. His voice rang inside my head.

"You will testify," he said. "Testify against the Jews who clutch at their foolish covenant until death and beyond.

Testify against those who would take the story of my dying and turn it into magic for their own political ends."

"How," I cried. I could hear my own voice echoing back to me. "I do not know how to speak, I am too young."

Yeshua leaned forward, almost touching my forehead.

"Do not say, 'I am too young.' Do not be afraid of them, for I am with you and will rescue you."

Then he reached out his hand and touched my mouth and said to me, "I have put my words in your mouth. Speak of the peace that can be found within anyone -- Gentiles, Romans, even enemies such as you have been. As you speak, you will pour out your own heart and you will be refilled."

His eyes offered absolute forgiveness. I began to weep. I wept for most of the three days I stayed with Ananias. Great sobs and cries of anguish, like a gutted animal dying slowly. At the end, I believed that I was forgiven, and I knew that I must earn that forgiveness every day for the rest of my life. Even if it cost me my life.

I have said that insight comes only slowly, and it did not come then. But sitting in Ananias' garden, I knew that I could no longer be part of the high priest's cadre. I did not have the teachings that Maryam would give me -- and of course it was many years before I could even understand and act on them. Years in which so much damage was done to Yeshua's memory and his wisdom.

It came to me that he had chosen me to be an instrument of his return. But who would listen to Saul the Persecutor? Surely not his followers in Jerusalem. I did not even know them, and any knowledge that they might have of me was of a wealthy outsider, a consorter with Sadducees.

As my eyesight returned and my mind cleared, I raised these thoughts with Ananias. He mentioned Yeshua's secret teachings, the *esoterikos,* although he did not reveal them. I began to speak, hesitantly at first. Ananias asked if my vision, as he called it, could have been the resurrected Christ. I said I did not know. I said that he came in the likeness of flesh, but I could not say more.

People arrived to question me. They were very suspicious in the beginning. Here was I, an agent of the high priest, and an outlander from the East as well. Elevated in class far above the simple people in Ananias' group. A former student of the great Rabban Gamaliel.

Why, they asked, their voices hard, would Yeshua select you as his vehicle? Why not his brother Yaakov? Why not Cephas or any other of his followers? Why not Maryam Magdala, who occupied a special place in his heart?

The small group of inquisitors, all men, came at me like a pack of wolves. They needed to retain their sense of having belonged to something special, something unique. What would have happened next I don't know. Maybe Ananias would have taken me to Jerusalem for further examination by Yaakov and Cephas and the remnant of Yeshua's original flock. But those who had been with me on the road, fellow agents of the High Priest, also knew where I was. They had taken me to Ananias after I was blinded, not because of his membership in Yeshua's fellowship – that was generally unknown – but because of his reputation as a healer. When they returned, I was still unbalanced. I spouted confusing words about Yeshua surviving his cross.

Word got back to Jerusalem that I was somehow changed or turned. Just that quickly I was judged to be a danger. The same men who had accompanied me on the Damascus mission were instructed to bring me back, or kill me if I refused.

Ananias made a decision. He took me to a man who sent me on to another man, and then to another – until I was safely out of the High Priest's reach. I left Damascus and went south into Arabia, to the stone city of Rekem. To Maryam Magdala.

REKEM, ARABIA [37-40 CE]

Rose-colored mountains loomed over the narrow entrance to Rekem. It had been a long walk from Damascus, more than twenty days along a trail that was crowded with heavily-laden caravans. I had set out alone, despite a certain amount of danger for a solitary traveler. But if there was danger I did not notice it and remained undisturbed.

I appeared to be a member of the upper classes, well-dressed, upright and prosperous -- perhaps a young Sadducee. But I was neither Sadducee nor Pharisee, neither Jew nor Gentile. As I walked, I felt empty and desolate. I was a small and inconsequential thing, a butterfly wishing only to be consumed in holy flames. I frequently stumbled, and my sleep, beneath a roadside tree or bush, was troubled. It was not always Yeshua's voice, or his face, or the touch of his palm on my forehead. Sometimes I sensed his kindness, and sometimes it was as if a desert prophet possessed me, fulminating against the sins of Israel. Once it was like the story told of Elijah on Mount Horeb: "And a great and strong wind rent the mountains, and brake in pieces the rocks before the Holy One; but the Holy One was not in the wind: and after the wind an earthquake; but the Holy One was not in the earthquake: And after the earthquake a fire; but the Holy One was not in the fire: and after the fire a still small voice, *qol dmamah daqah.*" Once I saw Maryam, saw myself reflected in her flashing eyes, felt the weight of her fingertips on my fore-arm.

I knew something of the Nabataeans. They had come from the east, in times older than time.   Trade – and their mastery of water – had made them wealthy. Their caravans carried metals and precious stones, perfumes made from the *libanos* and *smyrna* trees, and *asphaltos* from the Dead Sea.

I entered Rekem through a narrow, overhanging passage that in some places was not much wider than my outspread arms. Then suddenly the city opened in front of me, encircled by great mountains -- including twin-peaked Mt. Hor, where the prophet Aaron is said to be buried.

Maryam Magdala's home had been hewn from the living rock. Two of the same guardians I had seen in Galilee and Jerusalem stood sentinel at the entrance, their short spears at the ready. I said that I came from Ananias; one of the men turned and crossed a broad terrace where water bubbled in channels, filling deep cisterns. He entered the great house and returned with a dark-skinned girl who was barefoot and wearing only a short, almost translucent linen wrap. I followed her through a series of high-ceilinged stone rooms. Tapestries covered the walls and floors. Exquisite furnishings had been placed for both comfort and appreciation.

We found Maryam standing very still in a circular, brilliantly-lit inner room. Polished metal plates were arranged around the room, each as tall as a man. In Rome, many years later, Lucius Annaeas would call these *specula.* Hanging lamps suffused the air with light and the scents of frankincense and myrrh. I saw an infinite number of Maryams, reflected in all directions. She stood in the center of the room, facing a massive stone cube, her eyes wide and unblinking, her arms crossed in front of her. The cube was inscribed with arrangements of concentric swirls which seemed familiar to me.

The room contained two large pools. The first appeared to hold clear cool water. Steam rose from the second, misting the perfumed air. A large cushioned couch, covered in rich fabrics, filled a carved grotto. I later learned that Maryam's house had been designed so that this vaulted room was at its center.

Maryam was pale as white marble, unaffected by Rekem's desert sun. Her unbound red hair was like a living flame. An ankle-length sleeveless silk garment hung loose on her spare frame. She wore no jewelry. Once again, as in my memory, I had the conflicting impressions of youth and age.

She turned and noticed me staring at the pools.

"Greeks bathe for hygiene," she said with a welcoming but wearied smile. "Jews bathe for purification. Here we bathe for those reasons, and also for pleasure."

Maryam stepped near me and her smile broadened. I realized that the world had until then been incomplete, lonely and desolate.

"Welcome Saul," she said formally. "We have much to talk about."

She spread her arms to indicate the space around us.

"For me, this room is like the *Qodes HaQodasim,* the Holy of Holies in the Jerusalem Temple. This block of stone, brought here in the mists of time, represents Al-'Uzzá, a goddess of love. Did not Yeshua say that the first commandment is love?"

Maryam giggled, and for an instant she was like a young girl. She was enshrouded in a soft, living haze. Or maybe it was just the candlelight, the *specula* and the steam from the pool.

"I was conceived in this room, "she said.

Maryam linked her bare arm in mine. She led me out of the room and delivered me back to her waiting acolyte.

"You have been long on the road, Saul. Bathe, rest, and then we will talk."

It was near twilight when the same dark-skinned girl led me through the house to a wide terrace, where Maryam reclined on one of two matching couches; a low table stood between them. The table was made of some precious lacquered wood that reflected the last light of the setting sun. Maryam held a papyrus scroll in her hand, which she put down when we appeared. She gestured for me to sit across from her. The young woman bowed and left us. Another girl, almost a child, brought fruit and wine on a gold tray. When I was seated, Maryam poured the wine, which was somewhat bitter. She took nothing for herself. I noticed curious inlaid patterns on the pottery bowl, the wine jug and the drinking cups.

"Was it so long ago," Maryam said, "on the mount, next to the Sea of Galilee"

She did remember! I counted back.

"Seven years."

"What was your first impression of Yeshua?"

"He took me unawares," I said." There was something in his eyes and in his voice."

Maryam's smile deepened, although her own eyes were sad.

"That was his effect on everyone. It was almost a kind of sorcery."

"Sorcery?"

"He knew the ways of healing. Oils, laying on of hands. Using his voice as an instrument. But it was his uncanny calm, his certainty, that was the source of his power."

Maryam paused again. This time she looked away, and her gaze seemed to range far beyond the mountains ringing the city.

"I was born and raised in this house," she said. "There were many scrolls. From Jerusalem and Greece, and from Egypt and the east as well. I was taught to read, and to think and to question. I was traveling in Jerusalem when I heard about Yeshua. To me, as to others, he was an enigma, a question addressed to the world. What did he know about life and death, about living, that made him so compelling?"

"I only saw him that one time in life."

Maryam raised a perfectly formed eyebrow.

"He told us that the answer to living was beyond words, that words could only point the way, and not even directly."

"That is why he spoke in parables?"

"Yes, two messages. *Exoterikos* for those who can only manage one step at a time. *Esoterikos* for some initiates, or those, like you seem to be, with special sensitivities. But there was a danger in that. Once Yeshua had gone, clever men – and not so clever men --could draw conclusions that he had never intended."

"You mean Cephas and Yaakov?"

Maryam studied me carefully.

"They knew him," she said.

"But is this the way? What we hear from Jerusalem? That Yeshua is now the Christ, a Jewish Messiah come to fulfill the law and the covenant?"

"Saul, something in you was ready to accept him completely. From that very first day on the mount. It is what Ananias saw in you and it is why you are here now. Anger, or jealousy, are not part of that acceptance."

"But are we safe here?"

Maryam tossed her head, and her lush hair whirled around her face.

"Many gods are worshiped in Rekem," she said. "All, for the present, are welcome. And we who have chosen Yeshua's way are not interested in propagandizing others."

"Unlike those in Jerusalem," I said with some bitterness.

Maryam exhaled slowly, and I felt the warmth of her breath.

"If you stay awhile," she said, "your anger will drain into the earth like water poured from a cup."

There were others in Rekem who had known Yeshua. I was closely questioned, as I had been in Ananias' home in Damascus. The accents of my interrogators were from Egypt or even further, beyond my ability to identify.

Maryam led the questioning.

"You say you have seen him, Saul, in dreams. But there are more than a few of us who knew him in life, studied with him, learned as well as we could what he was trying to teach. Which is why, just as he was important to us, so are you important. "

I tried to explain that what had been absolute clarity during my blindness, had become confused.

I said, "A great light knocked me off my horse. I think I must have been stunned by the shock of hitting the ground."

Maryam searched my eyes.

"And then?"

"Darkness, absolute darkness. I was terrified, alone in all the world, when I heard a faint voice, far off, calling to me. 'Saul, Saul.' The voice became louder. I could feel my companions lifting me from the ground, even hear them speaking to one another. Concerned voices, asking what had happened to me. But I was struck dumb as well as blind."

An older man, dressed as an Egyptian, leaned forward.

"Did you see anything?"

"I saw … first I saw my parents. They were younger, as they were when I was a boy in Tarsus. I saw friends from that time, playing in the hills above the city. Then I saw Yeshua, when he looked at me that day on the Mount."

"When you were called," the man said, "and did not follow."

I stopped speaking, trying unsuccessfully to find reproach in his words. I was not ready to speak openly about my lifetime of visions. I recalled too vividly the look on Rebhi Gamaliel's face when he had interrogated me about my vision of the many-faced beasts.

"Continue," Maryam said.

But I could not speak. For a moment, it was just as if I was back there that day, listening to him. I could feel the wind coming off the sea, carrying his voice up the hill. I experienced the sun on my face just as I had that day.

Maryam's voice drew me back.

"What did he say? In your vision?"

I rubbed my hands over my face.

"If I close my eyes now I can still see him, and his expression is one of sadness, even disappointment. There was one thing that I could make out. He said, 'Keep on speaking, for I am with you.'"

I lived for three years in Rekem with Maryam and the others. In that time, I tried to process the flow of visions that came unbidden day and night. I turned my memories over and over, churning, creating an ever-changing, jumbled stew. I look back at my ideas from that time and I despair. A young man's certitude, held in a deadly grasp.

The members of Maryam's group encouraged me to share my visions of Yeshua, his peaceful face remembered from the Mount, his body twisting in pain on his cross. Once they knew I had somewhat of a classical education, they worked that vein like determined miners for tin or gold. I answered their questions as best I could, dredging emotion and thought from memory and from whatever is common and deep in mankind. This was during the day. Each night, Maryam would come and sit beside me, asking only that I present what I thought I had learned. I tried my best. I babbled endlessly about anything and everything -- sun, moon, the stars of the darkest night -- just to have her near.

Day comes swiftly in Rekem, even in the cool season. I was restless in the night, and left Maryam's house well before dawn. I sat down to think near a wide cistern in the center of a lower terrace. One moment, the stars were alive in a soft violet sky and then the sun engulfed them, reds and oranges and yellows filling the day with life.

Maryam appeared, wrapped in wool, her head covered against the chill. Here in her home city, revered, she was able to venture forth without her armed guards. She sat beside me and took my hand. Her face was earnest.

"The servants told me that you had gone out," she said. "I dressed and came out to look for you. I asked the watchmen, and they directed me here. What ideas are you wrestling with so early in the morning?"

"Maryam, was he the Messiah?"

She sat back and watched the multi-colored display of a new day dawning. I thought she might be disappointed in me.

"He was a man like any other," she said. "And also, not like any other. You saw him. From a distance, he was of average height, not remarkable. A poor working man. His hands were rough from working in stone and wood, his arms and back were strong."

"But did he ever claim to be the Messiah?"

Maryam's expression clouded and she hesitated again before speaking.

"Some of his followers wanted him to declare himself. They had heard his message of the Kingdom, but either did not want to believe it, or could not separate themselves from their own histories and the history of their people."

A breeze blew off the mountains. Maryam drew her cloak around her.

"It saddened him," she said, "that his own closest followers could not take the needed steps toward wisdom. He finally realized that if they still wanted him to be the Messiah -- even they, who had been with him for so long -- he could never at that time convince the masses who did not know him well."

She looked deeply into my eyes. I became lost in the flecks of gold that I found there.

"He made the decision to die," Maryam said. "He decided to fulfil the Messianic prophecy. He rode into Jerusalem on an ass. He allowed the people to briefly believe in him. He gave the people a Messiah they could understand --- someone who would be remembered. And he hoped that over time, those of us left behind could eventually spread his true message."

"But he was wrong, wasn't he? He is dead and gone – or just gone…. "

Maryam's gaze turned inward.

"Just gone, Saul."

"... and look at what his followers have done. They have turned him into an idol! What good did his time accomplish?"

Maryam smiled softly.

"We are here, are we not?"

I awoke one morning with a sudden thought that made me feel like a fool. I rushed to find Maryam. She had risen before me and was reading on a comfortable couch. A pitcher of water and some fruit lay within reach. She gestured for me to sit, and put down her scroll. She sat before me, searching my eyes. She did not speak.

"Yeshua's closest men were like him," I said slowly. "As you have told me, poor workers from the Galilee. Illiterate. None was a scholar, none had a home or wealth. Yet here are you, high-born, as were the women I saw around him on the Mount and at his crucifixion. And there at the cross were Joseph and Nicodemus, also high-born. As are the people whom I have met here in Rekem. Joseph was easily able to convince Pilate to free Yeshua from his cross after only a few hours!"

"What are you asking, Saul?"

"Yeshua clearly had two groups of people devoted to him. How else could he have walked around Judaea, followed by ever-growing crowds, feeding and sheltering them. Who bought the fish and loaves for his and their daily bread, who arranged shelter at night?"

Maryam studied my face. Although I loved and trusted her, I still believed that she was not going to tell me everything that she knew. She settled back against her cushions.

"Some of us, Jews and others, have been dissatisfied with our own people even more than with Rome. Yet we were unwilling either to take up the dark revenge spoken of in prophecy, or to give in and become as Roman as the Romans. Some were those called God-fearers -- Gentiles, again mostly wealthy -- who had learned to love Jewish traditions and culture, and who even followed some of the laws. Some were Roman citizens, scholars and free thinkers, for whom a man like Yeshua, no matter where he came from, was at first fascinating and then a necessary inspiration. I have told you that I heard of him and went to see for myself. Others found him as if by chance. Joseph says that Yeshua appeared one day in the Temple, just weeks after the Baptizer was taken and killed. He began speaking with a group of men who were waiting to offer sacrifice. Joseph was one of them. He wondered at Yeshua's prodigious knowledge and so he drew him away from the others and questioned him."

"What did he learn?"

"He said it was immediately clear that Yeshua had no education other than hearing the law read in the Temple, or perhaps in the small synagogue in Nazareth. But he had a complete command, as if he had never forgotten anything he had ever heard. And Joseph said that Yeshua's reasoning was greater than the wisest, most clever Pharisee. He mentioned your former teacher, Gamaliel. Joseph said not even he could have debated successfully with Yeshua. They say now that he was taken to the Temple as a boy, and that he asked the priests questions they could not answer. I don't know if that is true; so many stories have been told and retold."

Maryam drew her fingers across her brow.

"Yeshua began coming to different homes, always alone, and it was just as Joseph said – his grasp of the law was immediate and total, his memory perfect. He seemed like a trained scholar, not only in his knowledge, but in his tones, the words he used, the way he confidently combined them. It was as if a great power was speaking through him, as if he was only a vessel for something beyond himself. Yeshua said he had always known he was different. He said that the readings of the law in synagogue always seemed to be speaking to him personally. He would remember phrases, and questions came to him. He learned very early to keep his questions to himself."

"Why?"

"Everyone, from his parents, to the rebhis at synagogue, to his older cousin Yohannon, had what he called easy answers for him. Pharisees had one way of answering, Sadducees another, Essenes still another. Once we hosted a scholar from Alexandria, Lucius Philo. He was a Jew who tried to match Jewish laws and prophecy with those of the Greeks. Yeshua was initially fascinated by Philo, but in the end, it was the same."

"Easy answers?"

"Philo's ideas did not hold up under scrutiny. They were, as all the others, only partial answers, depending at base on unproven postulates."

Maryam smiled in memory and I wanted to fall at her feet.

"They call him Messiah now," I said, "even King of the Jews. Who did he think he was?"

"He rarely reflected on such things," she said. "I think he was conscious of being all things to all people; whatever they brought to him as gifts of their hearts..."

"Gifts of their hearts?"

"Yeshua said that we are all lonely in our hearts, wanting to belong to something beyond ourselves. Some came to him after hearing of his reputation as a healer and sorcerer; they wanted to be rid of illness, demons, sadness. Some came looking for a warrior Messiah, who would lead mighty armies against the Romans, who would re-establish an earthly Kingdom of Israel. Others sought a heavenly Kingdom, either angels coming down to purge unbelievers and offer immortality and joy to believers...."

She paused.

"Or what?"

"Or simple assurance. A kept promise, eternal life after this short, mean time on earth. I myself came to him because I was already experienced in the art of visions, and I thought I might learn from him."

Maryam reached out to place her hand on mine. I thought my heart would burst.

"My people are comfortable with dreams and oracles, Saul. Yeshua taught me to accept myself, to rest in my visions and so gain wisdom."

I told her then -- as I had never told anyone, neither Cleanthes, nor my father and mother, nor Rebhi Gamaliel –

all the interior details of my visionary life. My childhood terrors, the days wrapped in sweaty coverings, gnashing my teeth and twisting my limbs in despair. Seeing my own hopelessness reflected in the eyes of my parents and my sisters, the smug disdain in the voices of the Tarsan synagogue leaders.

Maryam stared into my eyes. She drew her full lips together in sympathy.

"You were born in the wrong place," she said, "even with your Stoic teachers. If you had been a child here, or in the east, elders would have known better how to help you shape your dreams."

"What do you mean?"

"Think of it. Your first remembered vision was of an angry male god, a statue on a temple. Your parents took you to the synagogue, did they not, for explanation? But the rebhis had no understanding of the great and gentle forces of nature – they had only their mighty Holy One, who kills and destroys. Little wonder that you learned to interpret your experiences as dangerous and even deadly. From Greek thinking you learned that there are no gods, but this was inconsistent with your experiences. Later, Rebhi Gamaliel tried to draw you into the violent visions of Ezekiel, with his *merkabah* chariots and many-faced beasts."

Maryam looked at me – almost – with pity.

"Where among the Jews," she said, "save in the *Âisma Aismátōn* -- which has these days fallen into disrepute – are the stories of life and love, kindness and forgiveness?"

In that instant I understood for the first time that my monstrous infirmity, earth-shattering, blood-spilling, had been permanently annulled by Yeshua's living spirit.

Maryam watched as the change took place. She nodded in satisfaction.

"The Day of the Lord," she said softly, "will come like a thief in the night."

Then she took my face in her hands, as my sisters used to do.

"Yeshua also told us: 'If those who lead you say the kingdom is in the sky, the birds will precede you. If they say to you it is in the sea, then the fish will precede you. Rather the kingdom is inside you and outside you. When you come to know yourselves, you will be known.'"

I was enchanted. By Maryam's words, by the heat emanating from her fingers. It was as if a spell had been broken, or a thundercloud had finally released life-giving rain.

"The Kingdom," she said, "is transmitted from one person to another. This is the only way, not by promises of victory or battles or deaths uncounted. We all have the innate ability to be initiated into the *zoe aionios,* the consciousness that is timeless, and beyond time. The process begins with love."

Something seemed to occur to Maryam then. She didn't speak, but she withdrew her hands, wrapped her arms around herself, and shivered. I wanted to enfold her in my own arms, offering warmth and protection. But it was I who needed to be protected.

"Yeshua believed that he wasn't important," she finally said. "He believed that the Kingdom was inevitable, that someday all men and women would recognize it in their hearts and live accordingly."

"When will this happen? Not in this time of a Messiah Christ, and warring Jewish factions, and Rome over all."

Maryam frowned, as if I was slow to understand.

"Release yourself from your desire to see the working out of things," she said. "That desire will prevent you from discovering each moment in the Kingdom and serving its purpose."

"What must I do?"

"What we all will do. Continue to work in the world, understanding that most people will not and cannot immediately follow. Most people live in fear. Fear of loss, of not obtaining our desires, finally of death – which we try to forget waits for all of us. He showed us, as did philosophers in antiquity, that an individual's living or dying is not important. In the end, it only matters if each brief life brings others closer to realizing the Kingdom within."

Another day, sitting with Maryam in her house. We were on a wide terrace, bathed by the setting sun.

"In Jerusalem, "I said, "the story is told that after being baptized by his cousin Yohannon, Yeshua went west of the Jordan River, alone, to meditate and fast. It is said that Yeshua found Satan there, a fallen angel, who sorely tempted him."

Maryam nodded.

"Yeshua told us that some months before, he had gone into the desert West of Jordan to either attain wisdom or die. He said he found a place shaded by a rock overhang, with some berries and grasses to eat, and a small spring. He forced himself to sit and think over all he had learned, all he could remember. And of course, he could remember everything, the law, philosophies, different commentaries and interpretations. Every conversation through his whole life."

"He survived."

"He said that he emptied himself – he used the word *kenosis* -- until he had visions, or dreams. At first animals came to him, lambs about to be slaughtered for sacrifice, then snakes, scorpions and huge insects. Then what appeared to be angels or demons, tempting him. Finally, he experienced images of family members and childhood friends – his mother, brothers and sisters, his cousin Yohannon. Cephas and Andrew, who would be the first to follow him. Yaakov and Yohannon, the sons of Zebedee. "

"What did he learn?"

"Tales for children," he said. "All of history, all philosophies, are only tales for children. Wisdom is not wisdom. God is in nature and nature is God. It is a mistake to have a covenant with a wrathful Holy One, who protects or punishes any chosen people on his whims. Yeshua said that such a god could not be the highest god, so he concluded that there is no god who will either answer our supplications or rain down punishments according to whim. All things happen, he said, according to universal natural laws which we cannot understand. We can either accept the unfolding of the world as it is, or not. If we do, we can be wise. If not, as long as we desire or hate, grab or repel, we cannot."

"But this is far from what he said to the people."

"He tried to find ways to teach starting from what the people could accept. *Exoterikos,* as I have explained to you. And in the end, he thought that his own death was necessary to carry on the process, the eventual emergence of his discoveries in the world."

"But look at what has happened. Rival factions all clamoring that they are his true heirs. Judaea under Roman threat."

"And none of them can be his heirs," Maryam said. "To him, wisdom happens not in or by factions, but individually, one person at a time. And Rome, or Jerusalem, or Rekem, are all equally irrelevant."

"And his death?"

"Yeshua said that once a person tastes wisdom, life or death no longer matter. That person, one with the laws of nature, is free."

"But they are saying that he rose from the dead."

"Resurrection is a fantasy, Maryam said flatly. "Yeshua taught that the world is an illusion, an incorrect way of perceiving. What people want to think of as resurrection is actually the uncovering of what is eternal in all of us, experienced as newness, or *metabolē*. I remember one morning Yeshua had been unusually quiet, and one of the men asked about resurrection of the body. Yeshua smiled sadly – it was as if he already knew what would happen to him – and he said, 'Those who say they will die first and then rise are in error. Instead, they must receive the resurrection while they live.'"

We often walked about the city together. Rekem at that time was nearly as large as Jerusalem, although it was richer and more luxuriant. I never became used to the deference people showed when they came near Maryam. Some bowed deeply, especially the women. Men -- of all stations -- stood straighter and kept their eyes respectfully averted. Only children were bold enough to look into Maryam's depthless eyes.

We had been talking about my visions.

"There are many of us who meet Yeshua in dreams," Maryam said. "More than a few. Each of us takes something of him with us, and as we live our lives, his love will radiate out to others, to oppressors and enemies as well as to friends. In Greek, *agape.* In Hebrew, *chesed.* We must believe, as he believed, that in some far epoch love will conquer – and only then will the Kingdom which is inside us all be expressed in the whole of creation."

"But I lose so much each time," I said. "I want to weep from frustration, or bitterness, at my stupidity"

"Be patient. Each one of us comes to the Kingdom with different ideas and different limits. Some of us are men, some are women. Some are Jews, others are Gentiles. Scholars and common people. Fishermen and masons, Roman centurions, even kings. Each of us has a small vision of the Kingdom, a tiny glimpse of it, clouded by the burdens of our lives."

"And he saw it all?"

"He knew how to dream himself beyond this world, even beyond himself as a single individual. He would sit peacefully and close his eyes. After a while he would have no awareness of us around him, of night or day, warmth or cold, hunger or thirst. And he did not remain there, for he had to return to us in this world in order to teach us. When he returned, he would be exhausted but joyous. He would encourage each of us to sit as he did, and dream, and wonder."

"Will he come again?"

Maryam turned and smiled in the manner that had become familiar. I was a small child again, asking questions whose answers were obvious.

"When you realize that he is already within you," she said, "then he will have come again."

One morning, Maryam and I followed a path that wound its way up one of Rekem's guardian mountains. I carried a goatskin filled with cool water. The wind was fierce, and it was almost unbearably hot at the summit. We found an area of shade and sat in relaxed company. I was still a young man, and slow to learn, though I sometimes think I have become no more wise with the passage of time.

"He didn't have to die," I said. "He could have hidden himself, or left Jerusalem."

Maryam glanced quickly at me, and then away. She started twice to speak, and twice caught herself. It was as if she was fighting a battle within herself.

"There is much you do not know," she finally said, keeping her eyes uncharacteristically averted. "Joseph arranged everything. He spoke to the general in charge of the soldiers; he arranged for one of them to give Yeshua the potion…"

I must have started, because Maryam turned quickly to look at me before resuming her distant gaze.

"Potion?"

"Did you see the soldier attach a sponge to a reed and place it at Yeshua's lips?"

I cast my mind backward to that dark day.

"I thought at the time that it was a strange act of kindness."

"Kindness! The sponge was saturated with *circaeon* and *opos*, two extracts that are familiar to healers. I have used them myself, and so had Yeshua."

I said, "As soon as it touched his lips he appeared as if dead. And then a soldier pricked his side with a spear…"

"And blood flowed. If anyone had thought of it, that flow proved that he was still alive. He was quickly taken down – it was twilight -- then carried to Joseph's villa, where we revived him. Did you never think it was strange that he was taken off the cross after only a few hours? Most condemned are allowed to rot, picked apart by animals, a warning to others who may offend Rome."

"How…?"

"Joseph went to Pilate earlier in the day. 'May I have the body of Yeshua,' he asked, 'so that we can take him down before the Passover and bury him according to our traditions?'"

"Why would Pilate agree?"

"Pontius Pilate was not above accepting a bribe. Joseph was a wealthy merchant, a leader of the Pharisees and member of the Sanhedrin. Nicodemus also was an influential man. "

Maryam picked up a small stone and tossed it down the mountainside.

"I have heard," she said, "that when Joseph went to Pilate, he asked for the body – *soma* – which means a living person.

Pilate gave permission to remove the corpse – *ptoma*. And so it was done as you saw."

"But his wounds. His palms and ankles, his side where the spear had pierced him."

"Yeshua, remember, was a powerful healer. His will and his mind were stronger than anyone can imagine. Once he was revived, he marshalled his own energies, and along with special salves and ointments, he recovered quickly."

"And then he was gone."

"Yes," Maryam said, with a resolute voice. "He was gone."

She shook her head slowly. I thought I saw a flash of anger in her dark opaque eyes.

"And it seems, "she said, "they all now say that they have seen him. It is only seven years and already those who make that claim are in the hundreds."

"You don't believe...?"

Maryam leaned forward and took my arm. As usual, I felt the heat that coursed out of her.

"It is not important," she said, with what I thought was a forced lightness. "He used to talk about lies containing truth. Even In self-serving lies there remains a kernel of his truth."

Maryam and I walked back down into the city, side by side, almost touching. She stopped at the edge of a well in a small square. A young woman was drawing water. Eyes downcast, she shyly offered us a drink. Maryam refused, but blessed her. The woman colored deeply and skittered away, bowing and whispering under her breath. I thought she said something that sounded like *Theonoe*. I was reminded again that in this city, Maryam was a princess, or perhaps something more.

One stormy afternoon, Maryam found me in a side room, puzzling over a Hebrew scroll, always a difficult task for me despite my years with Gamaliel.

"His mother is here," she said. "With his cousin, young Yohannon."

I stood up so quickly that I almost fainted.

"Where are they?"

"We can see them after they are settled. "

I don't remember what Maryam and I discussed in that hour, as the desert wind howled through her fine house. We were both anxious – for me this was new contact with those who had been closest to Yeshua. For Maryam, it was the rekindling of old friendships. I knew that she had not seen Yohannon or Yeshua's mother, also named Maryam, since the chaotic days immediately after the crucifixion.

"Where have they been," I said.

"In Syria, far to the North. Another community like ours."

I had never considered that there were other exiled groups.

"Why are they here now?"

"Everyone there has left, either for the East or toward Iberia."

A feast was laid for the newcomers. I recognized Yeshua's mother from the day of his crucifixion. She was a small woman, older but not old. She was still dressed as a Galilean peasant, wrapped in linen from head to toe. Her hair was dark and shot with gray. I sensed something of her son in the way she held her head, and in her liquid golden eyes.

Yohannon was far from the boy I had glimpsed at Yeshua's crucifixion. He was man-sized, with the beginnings of a ginger-colored beard. He had his cousin's eyes, although where Yeshua had projected a calm confidence, Yohannon's face was a mask of determination. He pointed at me.

"Is this the Sadducee?"

"This is Saul," Maryam said. "He is one of us, touched, as you may have heard, by visions of Yeshua."

"More likely a liar," Yohannon said, "and a spy for the priests or for Rome."

I hung my head. Maryam stepped in front of me.

"He has been examined, Yohannon. "

"And you believe him? The man who has killed our people?"

Yeshua's mother reached out to touch her nephew's shoulder.

"Ananias and others vouch for him," she said. Her voice, although couched in the accent of the Galilee, was smooth and strong, demanding obeisance. She was quite unlike a usual Jewish woman, subservient and quiet when men were present.

Yohannon acknowledged her words with a shrug, but when I raised my eyes to meet his I saw that he was not convinced.

"We will see about this man," he said, and he did not speak again during dinner.

One morning, alone on a high ledge near the city of Rekem, I had an experience which, through my own damnable ineptitude, has spread like a pestilence throughout the world.

After a lifetime of visions, I had learned when they were about to overwhelm me. When I felt the familiar disturbances, I lay back against the rock, closed my eyes and suddenly I saw Yeshua, together with a group of his disciples. At least I thought they were his disciples, since at that time I had seen only his younger cousin Yohannon and Cephas, he who would become my opponent in all things.

They were at table, and as was customary among the Jews, bread and wine were being passed from person to person. I saw that all the men were grieving in some form or another. Some had tears streaking their faces, one or two sobbed into their sleeves or dropped their heads onto the table itself.

Yeshua alone seemed calm. He wore the same firm, implacable expression I had seen above the Sea of Galilee, on that day when I refused him.

His voice came to me, then, as if we were both watching the scene and he was describing it to me.

"They are eating and drinking," he said, "in memory of our time together. Each time in the future that they share a meal, it will be as if they recognize what we have in common, the goodness inside our hearts and spirits."

Later, I told Maryam what I had experienced.

"You recognize this, do you not," she said. "From the gods and goddesses of your childhood home? Taken literally, this is the god who dies each season, so that the spring may come and the plants flower and produce fruit. Yeshua has given you a metaphor, a parable to offer to the Gentiles."

And so it was. When in future years I spoke among the Gentiles, I told the story of my vision, and through my own poor skills it was misinterpreted and taken as historical truth. But still, I did no more than this: I argued that each of us can find Yeshua in our individual hearts, and be like him, and live with and through him, in this ritual of remembrance. Never did I countenance what their sacrament, their loathsome Eucharist, has become.

Fact: no one, in those early days, accorded any special significance to a sacred meal commemorating Yeshua, nor did they at any time use the words Christians use today -- his body and blood consumed in remembrance. They could not. This would have been a double travesty to them, who still remained Jews, rabid followers of their law and their covenant. They were forbidden to eat any meat with blood undrained, and further, this was human sacrifice, forbidden by their Holy One in the story of Abraham and Isaac.

It is also a fact that no so-called Eucharist was ever observed in Jerusalem -- in the way it now is glorified -- before the city fell to Titus in the second year of the emperor Vespasian. But slowly, things changed, and the changes have calcified in the generations since. Gentiles became larger in number in the chorus of Christians. Without guidance, in their groups and homes, they turned Yeshua's memorial meal into a barbaric orgy. Participants were told to believe that they ate Yeshua's actual body and blood, and that through this act of anthropophagy they were saved. I take responsibility for this travesty, perhaps my greatest failing and my greatest sin.

The success of this Eucharist is additional proof of the opportunism of Cephas and Yaakov and their henchmen. As Jews, they were honor bound to refute such a diabolical rite, yet when it became popular in the east --- through the people's misunderstanding of my inept preaching -- they absorbed it easily into their Church in order to remain in power. Hypocrites! They defiled their own Holy One to gain worldly authority, not only over former Jews, but over the Gentile world as well.

After three years, Maryam and the others decided to leave Rekem. I pleaded with them, but they were obdurate. On the last night, we sat together on a high terrace, beneath the bright stars and endless skies.

"Where will you go?" I asked.

Maryam smiled her gentle smile.

"First to Alexandria," she said. "I will find a ship."

I dropped to my knees. My eyes filled with tears.

"May I go with you?"

"I believe you have many words to say in his name, Saul."

"But we can speak together!"

She shook her head, and her thick hair swirled around her face like a storm rising over the sea.

"I must go to the west. I must take his message of love to those who have never yet heard of him. Your mission is in the east, with the Gentiles and God-fearers."

"But what will I teach? Who will listen to me? I have not — except when he comes to me in a vision – any lasting feeling of wisdom."

Maryam abruptly stood up.

"Come with me," she said in a soft, uncharacteristically faltering voice.

She led me silently to the room with the hanging lamps, the *specula* and the stone cube. We stood facing one another and in the flickering light, Maryam's eyes blazed. I saw a richer purple flowing in the blue, and the golden flecks seemed to glow of their own accord. I remembered the tales of Cleopatra, last of the Ptolemies – how she had loved *sappheiros* stones, even having them ground to powder to line her eyes.

Maryam took my hands and spoke formally, as if reciting a prayer:

"Receive now this grace for me and through me. Become as I am and I will become as you are. Let the seed of light descend into this chamber, let it receive us as we open our arms in joy. Behold, Grace descends upon us."

She began to sing. Her voice was light and lovely:

"Awake, north wind, and come, south wind! Blow on my garden, that its fragrance may spread everywhere. Let my beloved come into his garden and taste its choice fruits."

Eyes locked on mine, Maryam released my hands and slowly shed her robe. I did the same, and we entered the steaming pool. We bathed each other, not speaking, and then she brought me to the wide low couch, where we lay together as if we were husband and wife. I knew again – and again -- the experience of *harpāzo.*

In the early morning hours, Maryam took my face in her slim hands and looked searchingly into my eyes.

"Here is your personal burden, my love. You are quick to take offense, quick to anger. The people you meet will often be the same. But we may not use anger to testify to love, no matter if others do. The more you fight with anyone, the farther you will be from any vision of the Kingdom. Yeshua said that truth could not emerge from sermons or from wars, from battling Rome, or through Messiahs rising. He said it might take a thousand years, or a thousand thousand, and that the passage of eras did not matter. 'Jerusalem will fall again,' he said, 'that is inevitable. And Rome will fall, and the empire after Rome, and the empire after that.'"

I wept openly. Fear possessed me, both at my own limitations and equally at the loss of her. I had no idea how to argue without intensity, which for me was anger.

Maryam smiled. She placed a warm fingertip on my lips.

"A new name will help," she said. "Saul the Tarsan will remain here in Rekem. We have washed him away with love."

Maryam darted her hand into a nearby stone jar, drew it quickly out, and touched my forehead with a few drops of cool oil.

"You are now Paul," she said. "In Greek, it means the humble one. So that you will always remember to remain humble in the name of love. "

She pulled herself tightly to me, as if surrendering us again to sleep. I listened mournfully to the soft rhythms of her breathing. Then she stirred, stretched and brought her lips to my ear.

"But the name," she whispered, "also contains the possibility of destruction. In Persian, Paul means the deceiver."

How I wish, all these years later, that I had been able to live up to Maryam's exhortation, that I had been able to fulfil her hopes for me. That I had been in any way worthy of Yeshua's gift – and hers. But it has been a long, long road and the false steps were many. Humble I have not been. And have I in the end been nothing more than a deceiver?

WANDERINGS [40-60 CE]

I have never seen Maryam since we departed from Rekem, nor heard a word about her or where she may be. I have remained, in her memory, a solitary man, *agamos*. But Maryam re-connected me with the boundless joys of love, and so I have inspired men and women to love as they can. I have had news of some of the others over the years. The two sisters from Bethany, Maryam and Martha, joined their brother Lazarus and settled in Iberia. Nicodemus went north into Pontus. And Joseph? He moved his business interests to Alexandria and began to teach, quietly. Some say that he appeared from time to time in Jerusalem to debate with James and Cephas. In later years, when I was in the north, I heard of a student of his, Terebinthus, who taught in Babylon, using the name Buddas. Before he died, he gave Joseph's books to a widow, who in turn gave them to her slave, a man named Cubricus, later known as Mani.

I went from Rekem to Jerusalem to confront Yaakov, Cephas and the others. "This is the Saul who persecuted us," some said, and turned their faces from me when I rose to give witness. More than once I was told to leave a gathering of believers.

I soon left Jerusalem and at first it was not much different for me. But slowly, attitudes changed. One day I was barred from the door of a home in a small, nameless town. Two men, red-faced and angry, were ready to do me harm. An old woman came to the door.

"Let him be," she said. "If we believe in the risen Christ, we must believe that he can accomplish anything."

She looked at me steadily.

"Christ can even turn an enemy into a friend," she said. "Let him enter, and let us all listen to what he has to say."

I never knew, in those days, what words or meanings would drop off my burning tongue. I would concentrate on the vision of Yeshua, always near at hand, and begin. Only afterward would I try to make sense out of what I had said.

Nevertheless, I became lost in my image of myself. I saw my anger at Yaakov and Cephas, my impatience with those in the churches, as righteous wrath. I was Amos railing at Jeroboam. I was Jeremiah, Samuel, Ezekiel, Isaiah. I told myself that I was their successor.

Over time, I took stock: I was neither a Temple Jew, with ties to one or another city faction. Nor was I a poor country workman like Yeshua's male followers. I came from the East, had been educated by philosophers. I was far more comfortable among Gentiles than Jews. I approached the law in Greek rather than Hebrew. And, like all free men of my home city, I was a Roman citizen. I had never spoken of this in my years with Gamaliel. After all, some Nazarenes, like Stephen, had already been killed for their hatred of Rome – and for the danger they presented to the high priest and the Sadducees who did Rome's bidding. I did not then know whether Yaakov and Cephas held onto their old belief in Yeshua as a warrior Messiah. If they truly understood him as the King-to-be of the Jews, then I would as a Roman citizen be anathema to them.

Maryam had told me that Yeshua spoke so that even the newest listener could take something away. But he had found a way to speak at the same time to initiates, messages coded into his sermons that only they could understand. I resolved to try to do the same. I thought I would be a Jew for the Jews in Jerusalem, referencing my training with Gamaliel, for the Pharisees were at least neutral about the Nazarenes. I would denounce my former alliance with the High Priest and the Sadducees -- those who actively sought to destroy Yeshua's remnant. I would speak as an eastern Jew to the Gentiles, and I would speak to them of the ways that they could experience full membership in his name and communion. I thought that if I ever had to confront agents of the empire, I would announce myself as a Roman citizen, and one who counseled others that there was no danger to Rome from adherents of Yeshua. Render unto Caesar, I would say.

I failed to comprehend, in those early years, that although I was becoming all things to all people, I had no deep understanding of Yeshua's truer message. I was more than an empty jar, I know that now, which when tipped over yields nothing. I had Yeshua's continuing presence, but I still did not understand. And it would take many years for the wisdom that Maryam seeded in me to take hold and grow. I was still a young man. I resolved to speak louder.

So I went out from Maryam to the Gentiles. Cephas, Yaakov and the others remained solidly with the Jews. I knew that I was only preparing the way, telling a story as one speaks to children, giving them what they can understand and no more. I don't know what the others thought.

How bitterly we fought, like vultures over a rotting carcass. We fought over circumcision, over full inclusion of Gentiles, over keeping the laws. Cephas and I even fought over whether any of us could share a table with Gentiles. But it was always, between me and Cephas and Yaakov, only about who was the primary caretaker of Yeshua's memory and legend. We ourselves were angry children.

Yet through it all, as Maryam had predicted, Yeshua's true message continued to spread, like a deeper current in a turbulent sea. I look back now and see it most in the strong women who preached in those early years, and in the married couples, like Aquila and Priscilla, who demonstrated in their daily lives – even more than in their preaching – that Yeshua's message of love, honest love in all its forms, was at the heart of the new covenant.

In the east I met people who, like Ananias in Damascus, wanted or needed to believe in a risen Yeshua. I found comfort among them in Philippi, Galatia, Corinth, Thessalonika and other places along my route. For many years I moved among them, always questioned about my experience on the Damascus road.

Men were sent to instruct the communities: do not listen to this liar who has had so many faces, who talks about things that never could be. Retreat into the Tanakh, into the practices and the law. Once Cephas himself came to Antioch, where I was living, to discredit me.

As the years passed, more people spoke aloud about a risen Yeshua. Most were still Jews, and so their understanding of him was set into a belief in the Hebrew Holy One of old. Yeshua began to be spoken of as the Son, who would be the Holy One's instrument of final judgment on all those who did not believe in Him.

About nine or ten years after Claudius was proclaimed Emperor by the Praetorian Guard, I returned again to Jerusalem -- against my better judgment -- to debate with Cephas and Yaakov. Yeshua had been gone for nearly twenty years, and there was much to argue about. Now it is said that we discussed simple matters: circumcision, meal-time rules and the ways in which Gentiles could be accepted into the Holy One's bitter covenant. Most people believe that Yaakov settled all our disputes at that time with a sanctimonious decree. But it was not so.

No. For them – and to my shame, for me – it was about dominion. Who would control Yeshua's legacy? Would those who newly believed in him continue under the covenant of the Jews, or would they abide solely in his new covenant, abrogating the law and welcoming all peoples of the world, now and forever?

I cannot say that the others did not know Yeshua's truth, but I will say that they turned away from it. In ignorance, in fear, in the unwillingness to give up their power. How we argued, day after day, spewing venom in his name, almost coming to blows. They were after all his first chosen ones, his kinsmen. They had grown up with him, worked beside him. But I had experienced him as the living Christ and they had not, whatever they say now. I had had Maryam Magdala to reassure me, to teach me, to enable me to absorb – and preach -- his true message of the Kingdom within.

Maryam: they do not acknowledge her to this day, though she was Yeshua's closest helpmate and partner. She always cautioned me to conquer my anger. I confess I never have.

I always felt I had to be more fiery than they. After all, at any turn one of them could say: "Who are you, who did not know him in the flesh? Who are you, who did not walk beside him, speak and listen in his presence, heal with him?" And last: "Where is your proof that he came to you? In the spirit? And no one else saw?"

These were powerful points, and very effective when debating in front of the people. It was my nature then to dispute demonstrating greater passion -- as if by volume and vomited words I could overcome any retorts.

Later, in other places, I learned to respond thus: "Who was with Elijah when the Spirit came upon him? Who witnessed the word laid onto Ezekiel's tongue? Who stood nearby when Jeremiah learned that he had been consecrated, even before he was formed in the womb?" This always gave me a moment's respite. And then, into the silence, I would thunder: "And where were you, any of you, when Yeshua gave up his life on Golgotha? If you believed that he was going to rise from the dead, why didn't you find your own crosses, joining him in death and, perhaps, resurrection? "

Yaakov and Cephas. The Nazirite and the hothead. Brother and friend of Yeshua, storytellers. The two of them always aligned, like two dead fish hanging from a pole to dry. The night he was taken, they ran like rabbits. While Yeshua hung on his cross, Cephas ran all the way back to Capernaum, on the Sea of Galilee. And after Yeshua was thought to be dead, Cephas emerged with the story that he had seen the risen Yeshua. He gathered some of the others, and together they began standing in the local synagogues: Capernaum, Chorazin, Bethsaida. "Repent," they said. "The Kingdom of God is at hand."

There had been trouble with the Jews of Thessalonika. I escaped to Berea, where I was for a time more favorably received. But the Thessalonians came to Berea, along with agents of Cephas and Yaakov, sent from Jerusalem specifically to beleaguer me. Friends took me to the coast and put me on a ship to Athens, where my comrades Silas and Timothy would later join me.

When I arrived at the port of Piraeus, I was stunned silent by the number of idols and temples to gods named and unnamed. I at last found the synagogue, and there I addressed both Jews and God-fearers. As so often in the past, I was not well received. Jews still wanted to think of Yeshua as risen in the body, returning at the head of an army of mighty angels; they lusted for the return of their land and their power. Gentiles who came to hear about Yeshua were generally responsive to the idea of his personal resurrection, but they mostly wanted to make Yeshua into just another Greek or Roman deity, outside themselves, to whom they could pray.

I was always more sympathetically received by Gentiles – because, despite my nominal Jewish status, I was more like them than like the Jews they knew. I was always clear: I was not calling for a political uprising. Despite what is said today about my writings and opinions, I taught that resurrection takes place in the heart. I wished fervently that all men and women could see Yeshua as I had, could hear his mighty voice, as I had, could be blinded off their feet and changed forever, as I had been. So when I preached before the Gentiles – and any Jews present -- I spoke of a Yeshua resurrected in the spirit. I did not speak about a bodily resurrection because I had not experienced it. But I also knew that he had come to me in spirit, in a vison, and so that is what I preached. Some caution was necessary, and even some casuistry, since Jews and Gentiles were found together in the synagogues. But by the time I got to Athens I had already traveled many hard roads, had only a stone many nights for my pillow, and faced more than a few crowds who clamored for my life because of what I preached. I had learned -- despite my natural tendency to speak plainly even if it was not to my advantage – to be all things to all men, as my father had advised me many years before.

Nevertheless, in Athens the well had already been poisoned. I was asked, "Did you know him in life? Were you one of the Twelve? Did he rise in his body or did he just seem to?" Voices were raised, I was pushed outside the synagogue, and the altercation spilled into the marketplace. Violence was in the air. I despaired; this was even worse than Thessalonika and Berea. What would my mission become, what were my visions after all? Were Cephas and Yaakov right? I thought of Maryam.

A group of Greek scholars, gracefully dressed and clad in rich sandals, stopped and watched with bemusement. The mob became more menacing. I thought I saw a Jerusalem face or two, and I expected at any moment to be taken out and stoned. But then the scholars surrounded me, locked my arms in theirs, and drew me safely away from the clamorous, cawing Jews and God-fearers. We joined a larger group of men, all Greeks, at a wide stone rock not far from the *agora* and the huge temple dedicated to Athena, goddess of the city. There they began to interrogate me about Yeshua -- his words, his actions, the manner of his death, the question of his resurrection. Although their demeanor was friendly, I knew that our discussion possessed many elements of a trial. I was not yet out of danger -- it was a crime in Athens to teach worship of a foreign god.

While I was considering how to respond, I examined the many small shrines assigned to local deities. One was dedicated to the Unknown God. Fortunately, I knew the legend, told by Pausanius and Diogenes Laertius, about how, centuries before, the elders of Athens had consulted Epimenedes of Crete when plague threatened the city. Epimenedes' solution was to order a herd of black and white sheep driven away from the Areopagus; wherever a sheep lay down, it was sacrificed. The plague diminished and then ended -- and memorial altars were constructed at each sacrificial site. These were dedicated to the Unknown God, *ne ton agnoston.* Years later, Lucius Annaeus would quote Vergil's Aeneid on this subject: *Quis deus incertum est, habitat deus.*

When the men were finally arranged around me, silent, I mentioned this Unknown God. I said that we were all praying to the god of Heraclitus: the *Pneuma.* I did not speak of the Holy One – or even of Yeshua – but only said the word *theos.* I quoted from Epimenedes, and also from Aratus, a well-remembered poet from my boyhood in Cilicia.

I have read altered versions of my time in Athens. It is said that I somehow convinced the Greeks that the Unknown God was the Jewish Holy One, and that I even brought some of them to Christ. Nothing could be further from the truth. Had I tried to do so, I would not have survived past the moment that I spoke.

Some of the men argued that this was babbling on my part, but others followed me and asked for more words. On the second day, several learned women came and participated fully in our discussions. All in all, I passed a few days peacefully in Athens, sharpening old skills which had lain unused since my childhood in Tarsus. When Silas and Timothy arrived from Berea, we left and continued on our journey.

CAESAREA MARITIMA [60-62 CE]

I came back to Jerusalem, at age fifty-two, to face Yaakov and Cephas one last time. They had made steps toward admitting Gentiles, though they hated me more than ever.

I debated with Yaakov outside the Temple. To my shame, when he attempted to strike me, I hit him and he fell down the steps and was sorely injured. Cephas was nowhere in sight, but after that the crowd wanted to kill me. I was rescued by Roman troops from the Antonia Fortress and that was the last I ever saw of Yaakov. Within a year, while I myself was a prisoner, he was accused by the High Priest, Hanan ben Hanan, and executed by stoning.

I was two years imprisoned in Caesarea Maritima, north of Jerusalem. If I had remained in the city, I am sure that Yaakov and Cephas would have had me killed. I was finally taken to plead my case before Porcius Festus, the governor of Judaea, as well as Herod Antipas, the tetrarch, and his sister Berenice.

Antipas was beautiful. He was long and gracile, with brilliant dark eyes, blond hair, brows and lashes and perfect teeth which he showed off by smiling frequently. His *toga praetexta* was made of rich linen, blindingly white, with a red stripe at the margins. He wore it casually, as if his power meant nothing to him. When I was led into the room he started at my simple *toga pura*, which I had made sure to acquire before my interrogation. Antipas had not known, it seems, that I was a Roman citizen.

Berenice, the subject of many rumors -- not least that she was her brother's lover -- was Antipas' equal in comeliness. Though she was younger than he, they appeared to be almost identical twins. Like him she was willowy, and she was long-necked as a crane. While Antipas wore his hair in the Roman style, cut short in front, Berenice's thick locks fell freely in waves over her shoulders. I tried not to stare – I thought myself long past such influences. She was wearing a white *toga*. It was not linen like her brother's, but was woven of the finest silk from the east. In the empire in those days – and who knows, perhaps still – only adulteresses and whores wore *togas*. A respectable woman would wear a floor-length *stola*, wrapped modestly in a *pallas* that covered her hair. Berenice's shapely arms were bare; I thought, instantly chastising myself, that she did not appear to be wearing even the traditional *tunica intima* beneath her robe.

Berrenice's fingers played excitedly with the hems of her garment. When I bowed through Festus' long introduction, her eyes, dark like her brother's -- but with more of a predatory cast -- roamed over me, assessing. Her small teeth bit her lower lip and her brows were knit in what I hoped was open-mindedness. She was famous in that time for being well-educated, a scholar in her own right despite her youth. She was a widow, having been married to the nephew of Philo the Egyptian.

What did she see? A man in the middle years, of average height, gray fuzz covering his head and an unruly beard worn in imitation of Israel's prophets. I was haggard from meditation, solitude and simple food, and stooped from working at the table they had provided me. In recent years, as my eyes had aged, I had begun to squint. My hands were ink-stained, as usual, and perhaps I had ink on my face as well, where an unthinking hand had scratched. It has always been my habit to write each day, and I had been called away while composing. It was likely a treatise, lost to time, intended as a defense of Yeshua and the commandment to love -- and which I'm sure would have been construed in Jerusalem as one more mad attack.

Festus did not know what to do with me. There was pressure from nearly all Jerusalem parties to have me judged and almost certainly executed. But as a Roman citizen, I had the right to demand trial by the emperor. Although this enraged the bloodthirsty Jews and Nazarenes, the Romans could not agree that I had done any wrong, and so I was sent, in the company of a friend, Aristarchus, and a centurion named Julius, to Rome.

ROME [62-64 CE]

We arrived in Rome, with our guards and protectors, in the eighth year of the Emperor Nero. I was assigned to a large house where Dáire, a king of Hibernia, was also a prisoner.

Dáire's people were called the Iverni. They had fought for many years against the Legions, first those of Aulius Plautius and later those under the command of Publius Ostorius Scapula. Captured by treachery from his own kind, Dáire was taken in chains to Rome, along with his young wife. He was condemned but allowed to address the Senate, where his speech won him not only life but honor, if ongoing status as a prisoner.

Dáire was a huge man, broad-shouldered and large-boned, with pink skin and yellow hair. I thought this was how Enceladus must have appeared, or Eurymedon and Porphyrion, giants who fought the Greek gods. Dáire 's eyes were almost colorless, like the frozen lakes I would see when I accompanied him years later to his homeland. He was close to my own age -- that is to say, in the early fifties. He always stood with his feet planted wide, as if at any time he might need to draw his great sword and initiate battle. His wife – her name was Aife -- bore two small children, a son and a daughter, during our time in Rome. Aife, unlike women I had known before, always carried a sharpened blade. I admired these foreigners. I admired their vitality, and their delight in each other and their children, even while under the Emperor's threat.

In our two years together, Dáire worked to convince Nero that he would be a stabilizing force for Rome if he were allowed to return home. He was aided by events that had taken place in Brittania a few years earlier. A local king, Prasutagus of the Iceni, fought the Romans to a standstill and then sued for peace. When he died, his remaining followers were killed and his daughters were raped by soldiers. But his wife, Boudica, escaped. She and her daughters, unlike Roman women, were warriors themselves. They built a new army, defeated the Legions across the length of Brittania, and tore down Camulodunum, Verulanium and Londinium. One hundred thousand people were killed in those cities, many of them former legionnaires and their families. Dáire argued that his return home as a permanent ally, if not a vassal, would serve as a hedge in Hibernia against any such actions.

He spent a great deal of time on this effort, often in the company of Lucius Annaeus Seneca, the Emperor's former tutor and present advisor. Lucius Annaeus was more than ten years older than Dáire and I, richly-robed, comfortable in his knowledge and place. He was a member of one of Rome's oldest and most powerful families. He spoke of senators and emperors as if they were not earth-shaking, god-like beings, but everyday men with the same foibles and limitations as anyone else. When we three were together, we spoke always in Latin: Dáire hesitantly, and me with the gutteral accent of the east, unpracticed since childhood. Lucius Annaeus was of course fluent, though his voice carried the soft tones of Hispania, where he had been born.

Except for the judgment that hung over Dáire and me like a dark cloud, our meetings were stimulating and even somewhat pleasant.

I did not have Lucius Annaeus' skills in rhetoric, which he had perfected in the viper-pit of Roman politics. But my early education and my time in Jerusalem with Gamaliel -- poor student that I had been -- together with so many years defending Yeshua against the vile ideas of the Jerusalem plotters, allowed me, I believe, to hold my own.

Lucius Annaeus spoke of his own teachers Attalus and Sotion, about his early years with Caligula, and his mentorship of the younger Nero. He was brilliant and shrewd, although his brilliance did not save him some years later when Nero decided that he had been part of Gaius Calpurnius Piso's plot. He was also curious; he posed barbed, detailed questions about my studies at the academy in Tarsus, and when he found out that I had come from Judaea, he began to interrogate me about that troublesome province.

We were amiably reclining, one bright summer afternoon, under a portico facing the *peristylium.* Lucius Annaeus had just asked why I came to Jerusalem as a young man, leaving all that I knew behind in Tarsus.

"My father wanted me to learn our own Jewish traditions," I said. "So he sent me to Rebhi Gamaliel, the greatest Pharisee. It was in the midst of these studies that I saw and heard Yeshua for the only time."

Lucius Annaeus had been carefully studying my face, as was his habit. He leaned forward.

"There is more to this, Saul, than 'learning our own traditions.'"

I hesitated, but only for a moment. Then I surprised myself by revealing my initial vision of Yeshua, and of the charge I thought he had placed upon me.

Lucius Annaeus waved a languorous hand.

"Everyone has visions," he said. "Including my housekeepers."

"I have always been plagued with dreams," I said. "I came to Jerusalem in part because my father thought Rebhi Gamaliel could cure me."

"What was Gamaliel's opinion of this Yeshua?"

"Rebhi Gamaliel was a studious man, a true believer in the law. He counseled patience. 'If this man is truly from the Holy One,' he said, 'then it will become apparent to all. If not, he will inevitably fail.'"

Lucius Annaeus pulled at his fleshy jowls, a gesture that frequently preceded the presentation of what he thought was a deep insight.

"I have heard reports that in Jerusalem – and even in Rome – some say this man rose from the dead. They call him the Christ."

"Yes, this is so."

"And your own belief?"

"I can only say that he has appeared to me in visions."

Lucius Annaeus sighed deeply.

"Your Yeshua was a man" he said. "Just as we are, Paul. Unique piles of atoms, held together for a lifetime, no more than that."

Dáire nodded his massive head in agreement.

"When we die, we cease to exist," he said. His voice was deep and somewhat harsh as he tried to shape the Latin vowels.

"It is said that he raised a man from Bethany," I said. "I knew the man, whose name was Lazarus. But I do not know if he was raised from the dead, or only healed of an illness."

Lucius Annaeus snorted. He turned to Dáire.

"Julius Caesar wrote of your people, I believe. And so did Posidonius. Are there not priests among you who are known as druids? Don't they, like Caesar, believe in the immortality of the soul?"

"There are those who lead prayer in the oak groves," Dáire said. "They sacrifice the white bulls. I do not know what they believe."

"Diodorus Siculus wrote that the druids are clever," Lucius Annaeus said. "They speak in riddles. Perhaps they are also magicians, like Paul's Yeshua."

"I know nothing," I said, "about whether Lazarus had actually been dead."

Lucius Annaeus waved his hands dismissively.

"But is it true? Any of it? In Hibernia, in Jerusalem, or in Rome? I have no stomach for sorcerers."

"I only know that they say he has risen. That some say he will lead a heavenly army against Rome."

"To what end?" asked Dáire.

"To restore the greatness of the Jews"

Lucius Annaeus smiled like a many-toothed tiger. This time he gave full reign to his laughter.

"Your Jews, I am afraid, are not long for this world. The Emperor's generals are becoming impatient. Too many resources go into Judaea, and not enough profit comes out. It may soon be more economical to send the Legions and to put an end to this problem of the Jews."

One summer evening, waving a fan to move the stifling air, Dáire asked me to describe the crucifixion of Yeshua. Lucius Annaeus was also present, and he looked sharply at me.

I told the story as I had seen it: the weeping women, the absence of his male followers, the moistened rag, the death-cry, the removal from the cross after a few hours.

Lucius Annaeus, seated at my right, pulled at his heavy jowls.

"But was he dead?"

I hesitated, and Dáire, reclining on my left, sat up straighter. Lucius Annaeus repeated his question. I still did not answer.

"Our friend seems to have lost his voice," Dáire said.

"Let us look at this another way," he added. "I have, unfortunately, witnessed many crucifixions during my time here in Rome. I can think of better deaths. I must say that your account is troubling in several ways."

"How so?" I asked, but my head was down and I would not meet their eyes.

"Paul," Dáire said, "I have never heard of a young, presumably healthy man being taken dead off a cross after only a few hours. "

Lucius Annaeus sagely nodded his head.

"There are physicians whose medicines can generate the appearance of death," he said. "Can this have been the case with your Yeshua?"

It was out at last. But I was reluctant to share all of what Maryam Magdala had told me.

Dáire leaned forward and placed his heavy hand on my forearm.

"We are friends here. You and I are brother-prisoners. Soon each of us, or both of us, may at the Emperor's whim be consigned to the cross or even to the fire. There is no time for partial truths among us."

So then I told them some of what Maryam had revealed, more than twenty-five years before in the city of Rekem.

Both of my friends seemed saddened by my revelation.

"They bribed the soldier to give him a special medicine," Dáire said, "and bribed someone higher up to allow him taken off the cross. And when the woman…."

"Maryam Magdala."

Lucius Annaeus narrowed his eyes as I spoke her name.

"She was a Nabataean," I said casually, "first cousin to the king, Aretas. And Yeshua's most trusted companion."

"She was far from home," Lucius Annaeus said.

I hesitated.

"After Damascus, I spent three years with her – and others -- in the city of Rekem. In Arabia."

"I know of these Nabataeans," Lucius Annaeus said. "Diodorus has written of them as well. They are warriors and traders, who roam the desert like ghosts. Their history is ancient and noble. If I am not mistaken, they serve the great goddesses of the east."

Lucius Annaeus appeared as if he wanted to continue, but Dáire interrupted.

"So she was a sorceress, this woman? A maker of medicines?"

"They all were," Lucius Annaeus said. "But who made the substance that was in the moistened rag? This Maryam? Or the men who took him off the cross?"

"I have another question," Dáire said. "Did he know of the plan to save him? Did Yeshua know?"

Both Lucius Annaeus and I snapped our heads around to stare at him. Dáire repeated his question.

"What do you think, Paul?" Lucius Annaeus said. "Though you were little more than a boy, you were there."

It was a question I had been asking myself since that long-ago day in Rekem when Maryam revealed the plan concocted by herself, Nicodemus and Joseph. It had never been told to anyone else, not to the other women, and certainly not to his followers.

I spoke slowly, trying to recall the moment after Yeshua sipped at the rag.

"I don't think so. He believed he was going to die, and he fought them with all his strength, though he remained silent even as they pierced him with the nails. Then they raised him and he suffered, and just before his last breath, he released a terrible cry. I thought his spirit had freed itself. I thought he was dead."

Lucius Annaeus tugged at his jowl.

"Could this have been part of the plan?" he said. "With or without your Yeshua's knowledge? To have him survive the cross and then be presented before the people? Imagine the panic, the riots."

I sat for a moment and saw again the gentle face of Maryam Magdala.

"Maryam loved him," I said. "And so did Joseph, whose tears I saw as he carried Yeshua's body. Yeshua was ready to die, but I think they went against his wishes because they couldn't bear his death."

Lucius Annaeus grunted.

"And so the would-be messiah lived. What then?"

Dáire's face was grim. He wore no sword in the home unless outsiders were present, but his right hand found its way to his waist.

"Your 'Messiah' either escaped Jerusalem in the dead of night," he said, "or his own followers made short work of him."

"And dumped his body in an un-named grave," Lucius Annaeus said, "somewhere it could never be found."

I was stunned into silence. This time it was Lucius Annaeus who touched my shoulder in consolation.

"A living Yeshua," he said, "hounded anew by the Romans, would not be able to organize quietly, speaking here and there of the amazing resurrection miracle."

"It is simple," said Dáire. "With a live body, there is no resurrection, just another job for the executioners. With a dead body, also no resurrection. But no body – anything can be said."

Lucius Annaeus came to the villa one day with a gaunt man of about forty.

"I have told Gaius Plinius about your visions, Paul," he said. "He has had some experiences of his own in that area."

Dáire and I had been sitting in the *peristylium*, enjoying the first cool breezes of fall. I realized that I had heard of Gaius Plinius Secondus. He had been born somewhere in the north, and was one of the wealthiest men in Rome. He was much in demand in the resolution of legal disagreements. I also knew that he held no official position – perhaps he thought, as I did, that it was not good for one's health to draw too close to Nero.

Wine and fruit were brought, and when we were all seated comfortably, Gaius Plinius leaned forward and began.

"A few years ago," he said, "I was a cavalry commander at Castra Vetera in Germany Inferior. I have always enjoyed writing, and so during the slow times I began a study of weapons that can be used from horseback. One night, drowsy from hours of effort, I slipped into a stupor. I awoke with a start, believing that I was not alone. Then I experienced a great light, blinding me, and from the light came an imperious voice that I did not recognize."

Gaius Plinius paused, seemingly overcome by his memory.

Dáire was staring moodily into his wine cup, as if he was occupied by thoughts of home. Lucius Annaeas gestured for Gaius Plinius to continue.

"It was the voice of an old man," Gaius Plinius said. "He claimed he was Nero Claudius Drusus Germanicus."

Dáire and I looked at one another with raised eyebrows, not recognizing the name.

"Quite a famous old Roman," Lucius Annaeus said. "A great military leader in the conquest of Germania, both on sea and land. Adopted by Augustus. Brother of Tiberius, father of Claudius and grandfather to both Caligula and Nero."

"I have never heard anyone speak of him," I said.

"He died over fifty years ago," Gaius Plinius said. "Long before I was born."

Dáire frowned.

"What did the voice say?"

Gaius Plinius gestured impatiently with an elegant, long-fingered hand.

"He asked me not to let him be forgotten. It's inconsequential, really. But what is important is the reality of his presence. I felt as if I was blind and unable to speak. In fact, afterward I took to my bed and remained in some level of that state for several days, neither eating nor drinking."

We were all silent, pondering Gaius Plinius' words. I thought that Dáire and Lucius Annaeus were studiously avoiding any glances at me.

"Have you dreamed before like this?" I said.

Gaius Plinius locked his eyes onto mine. He nodded as if he had assured himself of something.

"Since childhood," he said. "And you as well?"

I was not quite ready, on that day among friends in a Roman villa, to spill my life out for inspection.

"Come Paul," Lucius Annaeus said, "we have listened many times to your story of the Damascus Road, on a day long past..."

Gaius Plinius reached out and took my hand.

"Please, you must. I had thought I was alone."

I did not want to answer him. What profit was in an answer? What if this elegant patrician could have had an encounter as deep and powerful as my own? How to explain it? Certainly, the shade of some half-forgotten warrior could not in any way be viewed with the same majesty as my first vision of Yeshua?

I looked at Lucius and realized that he was following my thoughts. He smiled gently, but there was a hardness to his manner that I had not noticed before.

"As Lucius Annaeus has just reminded us," I said, "I had an experience that changed me forever."

"And forever changed the narrative about the man named Yeshua," said Lucius Annaeus. "The man some now call a god."

I believe I glared at him. Lucius Annaeus appeared to take no notice of my discomfort.

"Tell me, Gaius," he said, "do you think that the voice – it identified itself as Drusus the Elder, I believe you said – do you think the appearance of this voice means that Drusus had somehow come back from the dead? His ashes, I seem to recall, were placed in his stepfather's tomb at the Campus Martius."

Gaius Plinius did not answer. Lucius Annaeus began tapping his knuckles on the small table next to him, emphasizing each new point as he made it.

"If Drusus was reconstituted," he said, "then where is he? Did you ever actually see him? And if he could be – reconstituted – then why not others? Why are there not hundreds, or even thousands of venerable spirits appearing to impressionable young men all over the Empire? Why not Julius Caesar? Why not Augustus? Have they manifested to anyone, offered advice, begged for remembrance? Have we heard of this anywhere else, outside the maunderings of self-important priests and vestal virgins?"

I knew this was a test of my life – a test for my life. All three men looked at me.

"I was changed to my very center," I said. "And I am no priest or virgin. I lived it, and in every moment since I have lived with it. I have endured beatings, disgrace, and

138

contumely, but that moment has remained my driving force."

My heart was racing and my chest was tight.

"I cannot prove anything about what I saw. How can anyone validate another person's experience? Perhaps I am a liar."

"No one would call you a liar in my presence, Paul," said Dáire .

"Nor in mine" said Lucius Annaeus. "But I would fault your teachers back in Tarsus who must not have made you study the sage Socrates. Are you familiar with his concept of the *daemonium*?"

Like a thunderclap, my early studies came back to me. Socrates – and Plato as well – thought that dreams recaptured aspects of each person's day, but were also informed by an indwelling spirit that pointed to tasks undone, directions not yet taken.

"You are saying...."

"I am saying nothing of importance," said Lucius Annaeus with a shake of his head. "But let me ask our younger friend here just one question. After you recovered from the appearance of the light and the voice, Gaius, were you changed in any way?"

Gaius Plinius held his face in both hands. His expression was one of incredulity.

"Yes, of course," he said. "I had been working on my cavalry study, but I abandoned it immediately and began my history of our wars and battles."

"A course of action," Lucius said, "you have followed with all-consuming ardor and effort ever since, even to the detriment of your practice of the law. You have been true to your vision."

Our conversation drifted after this last exchange. Out of kindness perhaps, or the respect good men have for one another, no one was willing to carry the point any further. But in the privacy of my heart, a seed had been planted and taken hold.

What if my experience of Yeshua was only my own *daemonium* – my personal small voice – urging me indirectly to change my life's path? What then should I make of all the years loudly preaching Yeshua's message? What had I actually experienced that day on the Damascus Road? What *daemon* comes to me still, in the loneliness of night or the life-giving light of dawn? Maryam, help me.

It was an afternoon in early spring. We three sat, as we often did, in the *peristylium.* We were surrounded by roses, lilies and various herbs, all filling the air with the scents of life emerging. The clouds above promised rain.

Dáire reclined on a low couch, almost hiding it beneath his bulk. He seemed at peace; he had had recent official conversations which led him to believe that he and his family would soon be going home. From within the house, we heard his two children giggling and screeching at their play. A servant appeared with goblets and a silver flagon containing dark wine

Lucius Aennaeus smiled at the happy domestic sounds. He reached for some wine.

"I have been thinking, Paul, of your Christians. Especially the man, Yeshua. I am coming to the conclusion that he was the most dangerous man who ever lived."

"He was only one man."

"Ah, but he is the inheritor of the Hebrew idea. Long after the empire has destroyed the Jews and their city – as they soon will, if my sources are correct – people will remember the threat implicit in this man Yeshua."

"Threat? But he was a man of peace. He spoke only and always of love."

Lucius Annaeus paused to sip at his wine.

"Tell me again," he said, "how your people, the Hebrews, came to the land of Judaea."

"The Tanakh says that they escaped from bondage in Egypt, wandered in the desert and then crossed the Jordan River...."

"Where they slew or enslaved all who stood before them. Every last nation, am I right?"

"They were...."

"The chosen people of their god. I know. So the land they took in blood was theirs by right, is that not what their holy book says?"

"It says that the land was the Holy One's land, as he was the ruler of all lands. He granted it to the Hebrews, and yes, then it was theirs by right."

"And any man already living there, believing it was his, had been his from time beyond time -- that man was wrong?"

"According to the Tanakh."

"Why would the Hebrews not do as the Romans, trade with conquered people, turn them into partners, convert them? Is that not how you have told me that your own people, in a far-off land, became Roman citizens?"

"That is not what the Tanakh says to do."

"No, Lucius Annaeus said sadly, from what you have told me, that god of theirs was bloodthirsty, constantly unforgiving, without love of any kind. Why, he nearly destroyed his most faithful follower, what was his name?

Job? The man who had all his family and fields and possessions taken away on an impulse?"

"But returned," I said.

Lucius Annaeus caught Dáire's eye. Our friend roused his great bulk and turned to look coldly into my eyes.

"If I was defeated in battle," he said, "and forced to kneel before another king -- forced to watch my family slaughtered, wives and sons and daughters -- what do you think I would wish for with all my heart, even if that king changed his royal mind and gave me possessions anew, different brides and children?"

"I have never had a family of my own" I said.

Dáire made a chopping gesture with his slab-like hand.

"I would await my chance, Paul. I would plot. In my heart I would see my fallen family, their bleeding bodies, every moment of my life. I would never weaken in my resolve. And when I could -- the first moment that I could -- I would spill the blood of that cruel king, and die happily in so doing."

"But the Jewish Holy One is no king. The Jews — and Christians — believe that he is the creator and ruler of the whole world."

This was the admission Lucius Annaeus had been waiting for.

"And thus he is the mold from which they spring? Is that not right, Paul? They act in imitation of him? "

"Yes, but the man they revere, Yeshua – he was gentle and kind."

"These Christians began as Jews," Lucius Annaeus said. "They do not remember the man whom you saw as kind and loving. He is now their soon-to-come warrior Messiah, son of their Holy One, and if they ever reach power, they will once again decide that they are approved to kill anyone, anyone at all, men, women, children.

"Men have always killed each other," I said.

"And excused their killing by appealing to honor, or need, or revenge. Or as in the Greek tales, when they were tricked by the gods. But even the Greek gods were changeable, now favoring one race and now another. This Holy One of the Jews – according to them, he is the universal god of all things, all men and all times. And yet for some unknown reason, he selected a pitiful group of former Egyptian slaves as inheritors of the entire earth and the heavens? Why did they deserve this favored status?"

Lucisus Annaeus shook his head.

"Try to place the gentle memory of your Christ atop this pretentious edifice, Paul. After Yeshua, they can kill – following their Holy One -- while at the same time speaking words of peace and love. The Jews, in their newest incarnation as Christians, are a poison which may well infect the entire world. The may make the Legions look like children at play."

I lowered my head into my hands and wept. But Lucius Annaeas, having begun the bloodletting, was in no mood to stop.

"Surely, Paul," he said, "your boyhood teachers did not neglect to mention Plato's concept of the *dēmiourgos?*

Dáire shook his head like a disdainful lion.

"What is this *dēmiourgos?* Some new weapon?"

Lucius Annaeas smiled thinly.

"Perhaps the greatest weapon of all," he said. "An idea. Indeed, Plato believed that the creator of the world was only an under-god, infected by the material nature he created, only partially filled with spirit. And though all-powerful over material things, he was an angry, mean and spiteful god, hateful of his own creation."

Once again, it was as if scales fell from my eyes. I thought: if the Jewish Holy One is the *dēmiourgos,* even if he is only an idea created by men, then his childish, threatening bitterness, his random cruelty, make sense. It was he who had made the deadly covenant with Moses and the Hebrews, he who had punished Adam and Eve. And it was the idea of this *dēmiourgos,* the false father, that Yeshua had rejected for all time. It was the good god, the unknown, unknowable god, above all things, in and of all things, who was the foundation of Yeshua's new covenant. Of his Kingdom.

Lucius Annaeas leaned forward. His face was wreathed in sadness.

"You have engaged on a difficult journey, my friend. But perhaps your Yeshua spoke a deep truth. Remember Epimenedes, who said, 'In him we live and move and exist.'"

I did not sleep that night, although the spring rain beat a hypnotic melody on the tiled roof above my head. In my life, I had heard of Greek gods, Roman gods, gentle goddesses and the warrior gods of many races. I knew that people worshiped gods who dwelt in springs, in oceans, in forests and in pastures. There were also gods who were said to appear as goats, wolves and horses, as well as men and women. But all these gods, even if sometimes immortal, were limited. They lived, just as men and women, under a set of universal principles. My Tarsan teachers were not united as to whether gods were real in any way, or just metaphors of the human condition. In the academy, I had been taught the concept of a creator, but it was a principle rather than a personality – an ordering of the world, an organization of laws. I was taught that although the world was difficult, it was not capricious. Wisdom lay in learning the nature of things and accepting natural processes.

According to Lucius Annaeus, the Hebrews of old had brought a new idea foaming into existence. Their Holy One was all powerful, beyond previous concepts of gods, and also like a rampaging father, all-vengeful. His world was a dangerous place, based not on laws of nature but on appeasing him and his ever-changing moods. The Hebrews learned from their idea of Him, and had used their supposedly favored status as a universal justification for their own rapacious behavior. They could always expect His blessing when they incinerated or disposed of any and all lesser peoples -- and all other peoples were by definition lesser, since they were not the Holy One's chosen people. There was also danger for the Jews in the lessons of the Tanakh: if the Hebrews were not as bloodthirsty as their god, He would surely turn on them. It was not, I thought, that the Romans were not cruel. But the Romans acted out of necessity, or practicality, or sometimes – as with Nero – out of whim. They did not appeal to universal precepts when taking lives. Lucius Annaeus said that the Hebrews were the first people who only had to look to the actions of their perfect god to see how they should behave, and who could then call themselves perfect as well. The Christians? They were powerless now, hunted and harried. But what if they ever gained power? Would they not then kill out of revenge, or even baser motives, and congratulate themselves for acting just like their god? It was all so far from the man who spoke that day on the Mount, who asked men and women only to live and to love.

HIBERNIA [66-110 CE]

I recently heard, here in my northern exile, a new story that has been passed around Christian groups from Rome to Brittania. Cephas and I, it is said, at the last became friends! Apparently, I admitted my errors and came over to his way of seeing things. And then the inevitable self-aggrandizement: Cephas was crucified at Nero's explicit instruction. How many ways can this statement not be possible? Cephas was not a Roman citizen. Only citizens, except for captured kings, could come before the Emperor in judgment. And the wait was – as I can attest – many years.

What probably happened: Cephas ran – as he had on that Passover morning so many years before—to preserve his miserable life. Could he have skulked away to live incognito forever? I doubt this even as I write – Cephas's self-importance would require him always to be the first of many, the final voice. He could never have accepted a humble, quiescent life of prayer, meditation and devotion. For so long, the fortuitously absent Yeshua had been his food, his drink, his lodging -- and his only cause for fame or status. Cephas might run, but he would run somewhere that people could adore him in the reflected glory of the Yeshua he had created.

No. More likely, Cephas was caught up in one of the constant Roman street sweepings and hacked to pieces – anonymously – like any other scab-ridden dog.

It has also pleased me over the years to hear of the many ways I met my own fate: burned as a human candle at one of Nero's fêtes; torn to pieces in the Coliseum; beheaded by a centurion whom I insulted in the street. I admit that this last invention is my favorite – it sounds like something I might have done.

The mysteries surrounding my own disappearance have a more commonplace explanation. Dáire finally had his audience with Nero, after we had lived together for two years. He gave a reasonable account of himself, swore allegiance to Rome, and was freed to return home. We had become friends, and so Dáire asked the Emperor if he might relieve Rome of my noxious presence. Surely, he said, I could cause no trouble to anyone from a hovel in the frozen North. Lucius Annaeus was still in Nero's favor then. He also counseled for my freedom, and so it was that in my fifty-fifth year, riding an ass, and in the company of Dáire, his family-- and a contingent of hulking yellow-haired titans who had travelled from Hibernia to escort their king home -- I turned and watched the Roman hills recede behind me.

After we left, it all became an inferno. A fire started in Rome and turned into a conflagration. Nero used this as an excuse to round up all of Yeshua's followers. Death and the most unimaginable tortures became commonplace. Then, after Nero was forced to commit suicide, Vespasian decided he had had enough of the Jews, and sent his son Titus to destroy Jerusalem. To this day, the killing has continued. They call it martyrdom now, and some believers are beginning even to court their own deaths. They have absorbed the outer teaching, and shifted it only slightly. Instead of waiting for Yeshua to come, they are eager to go to him.

We travelled for many days by land, slowly but steadily ascending into a range of rolling hills. After we passed beyond these — I learned that they were called the Appenines — greater mountains emerged. They were massive beyond imagining, covered in many places with ice. They seemed to pierce the very heavens. I shivered constantly in the deepening cold, while Dáire's people greeted the weather as an old and trusted friend. They laughed into each other's faces, their breath visible in the frigid air. Eventually we began to descend on twisting narrow pathways. Pebbles kicked by our feet dropped into bottomless chasms and I was continually certain that we would meet our doom. Finally, we came to a series of lakes which formed the headwaters of a broad, swift-flowing river. It was there that we stopped to build a ship.

Dáire's men had previously traded with natives of the region, and had processed and stored a great number of animal skins. Now they foraged in the nearby forests and came back with many stripped tree branches. The largest of these they pounded into the ground and tied together. The wood was of some type that bent readily without breaking; I gradually began to see that the boat frame resembled an upside-down basket. When I questioned Dáire, he only smiled.

After the frame was strongly woven with branches from the same flexible tree, the skins were sewn together, fastened to the frame and waterproofed with tar made in an oven from another type of tree. I was familiar with this process from watching my father's ships sealed back home in Tarsus.

When the ship was completed, it was cut away from the ground and turned over. Now the men took thick oak trunks and split them to make seats, cross-braces, oars and finally two tall masts. Additional skins were sewn together to create sails.

On the day before we entered the river, Dáire and I walked along the shore in companionable silence. His men sang while they completed their tasks, their voices rising and falling with the rhythm of their tools. Two of Dáire's younger kinsmen maintained a respectful distance behind us, reminding me that this river formed the boundary of the Roman Empire. Beyond it to the east was the unknown.

"In a few days," Dáire said, "we will reach the sea. Many years ago, brave men journeyed across that wide sea, even beyond my home, and returned."

I smiled.

"I have heard your men speak of Tír na nÓg," I said. "They say it is how the old ones – older even than you and I – pass their time frightening the children."

Dáire shook his head.

"We may not be able to see that distant land, he said, but it is there, beyond the curve of the sea."

I turned to him in surprise.

"Surely you have not read the Greeks, who proved that the earth is round?"

Dáire sniffed derisively.

"Paul, my friend, one does not have to read to know things. Do you recall what we saw when we passed beyond the first range of mountains, following the bright star toward home?"

"We arrived at a great forested plain. We could see no end to it, as if it went on forever."

Dáire nodded.

"And yet, within a few days' march the greater mountains gradually appeared. How was that possible? It can only be that the land curved toward us as we marched, and so I suppose that the sea must do the same. The earth must be round, or at least it is not flat."

We went into the river on a cold spring morning. The current was strong and the oars were not necessary. After a few days, I became used to the bending and creaking of the ship, understanding at last that its flexibility was its greatest strength. One morning, we stopped on the western bank of the great river. While the younger men were hunting game, I found Dáire in a pensive mood. He was staring at the dark forests on the opposite bank.

He pointed with his broad hand.

"There," he said, "in the time of Augustus, three Legions were destroyed."

The thought of anyone defeating, let alone destroying even one mighty Legion was inconceivable to me.

"How can this be?"

Dáire smiled wistfully.

"Two generations ago, a young man was captured by Rome and held for ransom. His name was Hermann, or in Latin, Arminius. He was clever, strong and brave. Over some years, he gained the trust of the Romans; he became a soldier, and then an officer. He was assigned to a commander named Varus, who was charged with extending Roman sovereignty over those lands you see there across the river. Hermann waited a long time. He made secret plans with local chieftains. He set a trap for Varus and the Legions. A false report came, saying that those chieftains were gathered in rebellion. Varus decided to crush them once and for all – he was a proud man, and Hermann had anticipated his response. The three Legions came, and they reached a narrow pass, with a swamp on one side and low hills on the other. They could only walk in narrow formation, spread out for miles. It was then that the chieftains attacked from behind earthworks they had built into the hills."

Dáire smiled grimly.

"I have been told that the sky rained spears. Many Romans died before they knew they were under attack. They were unable to organize themselves into battle formations, and when the chieftains came over the earthworks, they met soldiers fighting not as an army, but as individuals. Even legionnaires are just men, after all; many turned and fled, and were lost in the bogs."

"So what happened?"

"Those three Legions were the 17th, 18th and 19th. Our friend Lucius Annaeus told me that by Augustus' order they have never been reconstituted. Varus fell on his sword. Other Legions were eventually sent, and their revenge was terrible, but the point had been made. Augustus declared that this place, where we stand, was to be the final border of Roman power in Germanica."

We ate well that night, and the fire seemed to roar higher and warmer than ever. Within two weeks, we reached the mouth of the river, and faced the great northern sea. It was dark, almost black, cloudy and froth-capped, terrifying to me even though I had many times sailed the blue seas of home.

Dáire clapped me on the shoulder.

"Now you will truly see," he said, "how clever are our shipbuilders."

We spent twelve days and nights on the open sea, landing only once, on a strange headland with white chalky cliffs, to hunt and to obtain fresh water. Dáire and his people seemed to gain energy as we drew ever closer to their homeland. The oarsmen seemed tireless, hurling joyous insults at the wind and the sea. As for me, I lay wrapped in damp furs, convinced that I would not survive.

One sunrise, jagged cliffs appeared, a long forbidding wall that jutted straight up from the sea. The men cheered and increased the cadence of their oars. We passed the cliffs, laden with seabirds, and landed on a rocky beach. I thought at first we were on a beautiful green peninsula, but this was in fact the largest of a series of islands. Dáire ruled here and drew fealty – or at least respect -- from chieftains on the mainland to our east. Phoenicians and some Jews lived among the local people, who were all blond or red-haired, kind and poetic in nature. Like Dáire and his men, many were gigantic in size. The Jews worked in tin mines, trading for goods brought by ship from all over the Empire. Their leaders knew Joseph of Arimathea, and one even said that my father's name was familiar to him. They were not like Pharisees or Sadducees, enmeshed in the deadly partisan politics of Jerusalem and Judaea. They reminded me of my parents and cousins back home, living lives of quiet confidence and joy, following their law not as slaves but as believers freely choosing. Many had intermarried with Dáire's people, and over time had absorbed some of the islanders' beliefs into their worship. When I told them of my visions of Yeshua, they easily coupled belief in him with legends of local gods.

I had been five years in the North. The cool season had returned, bringing chills into my bones that no fire could banish. One morning Dáire came to the stone hut he had provided for me. He brought with him, under guard, a thin, disheveled, wild-haired native of Britannia, one who called himself a Christian. Dáire had told this man that I was an elder of his people, a venerated scholar who could read and speak, somewhat, in the languages of the east. The man was distraught, although it did not seem as if his discomfiture was new, but rather that it had grown over time to possess him.

I rose and offered the man a bearskin to wrap himself in. One of Dáire's warriors presented him a warm bowl of coirm, a local beverage made from barley. The man refused both, although he was shivering from the cold. His eyes were burning, and he seemed to see far beyond the room in which we found ourselves.

"This is no time for comfort," he said in poor but intelligible Greek, speaking to me alone. I thought I caught a whiff of Yaakov, the permanent Nazirite.

"I have taken it upon myself to tell the whole world what has happened," the man said. He glared at each of us in turn. "The Romans have destroyed Jerusalem! We will all soon be with Christ!"

Dáire stroked his beard, which was still flaxen though he was past sixty. He caught my eye. This was only what Lucius Annaeus had predicted.

The man uttered a joyous bark and began to babble.

"Let me be food for the beasts," he shrieked, "through which I can attain to God! I am God's wheat, and I am ground by the teeth of wild beasts that I may be found pure bread of Christ. Rather entice the wild beasts, that they may become my tomb and leave no trace of my body, so that when I fall asleep I will not be burdensome to anyone... I long for the beasts that are prepared for me, and I pray that will be quick with me. I will even entice them to devour me quickly... Fire and cross and struggles with wild beasts, cutting and tearing asunder, rackings of bones, mangling of limbs, crushing my whole body, cruel tortures of the devil, let these come over me that I may attain to Jesus Christ!"

I said nothing, and the man — his name was some self-constructed amalgam that must have been meant to mean "Child-of-Christ" — scowled, as if seeing me for the first time.

"Are you not the one they speak of, in Britannia and even as far as Germania? The one who came from Rome and the east?"

I smiled thinly.

"I am no one. I am a *monachos,* of no importance to anyone. I serve my friend and king, Dáire of the Iverni, who stands here before us."

The man squinted at me as if to clear his vision. Then he shook his head, turned to Dáire, and switched to the language of Hibernia, which he spoke no better than he did Greek.

"It was more than a year ago," he said. "The legions came, under Titus, and camped outside the city gates. Many people, so many, ran out, begging for mercy."

Dáire maintained a stolid face.

"And was mercy shown?"

The man gaped at him.

"Mercy? They were put to the sword, or crucified in their thousands. And then the legions entered the city. Men, women and children, the old and the young, were butchered outright or taken as slaves. But that was not the worst of it."

"How can that not be the worst?" Dáire said quietly. "Slaying innocent women and children?"

The man started to respond intemperately, but then seemed to recall that he was addressing a king.

"The Temple was rent stone from stone," he said. "His voice rose into his throat and he was almost weeping. "The Holy of Holies, where the Holy One, Blessed be He...."

Dáire glanced casually around the room. His warriors noted the signal and gripped their swords. The man continued in a torrent of words.

"....it was utterly destroyed by the invaders."

"Then the prophecies have been fulfilled," I said softly, and the man whirled to stare at me. His mouth hung open.

"What do you --- what do you know of prophecies?"

"Is it not written that if the chosen people do not follow the Holy One's commands, they will be destroyed? How many of the prophets made such predictions?"

The man stood mute as if he had been struck.

"And I have also heard," I said, "that even Yeshua, when he was being led to his cross, said much the same thing. For what was Yeshua if not a prophet himself: 'Then they will begin to say to the mountains, fall on us, and to the hills, cover us. For if they do these things when the tree is green, what will happen when it is dry?'"

The man, "Child-of-Christ," pointed a bony finger at me.

"Who are you to speak His name? You? A demon-servant of these cursed savages?"

He plunged his hand into his robe and drew out a short knife. I believe it was his intention to attack me, but he did not complete a full step before he was cut down.

We were all standing. We stared at the corpse. Dáire gestured to his men.

"Take this Christian away and leave his corpse for the wild beasts. As he so devoutly wished."

When we were alone, Dáire stood near the hearth, his back to me, warming his hands. He picked up a large iron pole and effortlessly stirred the logs. When he spoke, his voice was a pronouncement of doom.

"So your Jerusalem is gone," he said. "War begets war. Death begets death."

He turned to face me. His immense body blocked the firelight so that he spoke to me in shadow.

"This man lived – and was willing to die in self-righteous anger – for Yeshua, the Christ? Better that no more of these people come into my lands."

"Those still alive seem to look for death," I said. "As if in following Yeshua to their own personal crosses they can enter his Kingdom."

Dáire did not respond. Perhaps he did not even hear me. He turned and went out into the cold.

That night I thought of all the wars. Jerusalem and the Temple, destroyed. What now could be said of the Holy One's chosen people? How would this devastation be interpreted? And of course, I already knew. It had been foretold by the desert prophets. When the Seleucid king of Babylon destroyed the First Temple, they said that the Holy One had turned against his people, punished them for incomplete submission. So it would be again. But what role would Yeshua play in future sagas?

More than eighty years have passed since I watched them take Yeshua off his cross, and I have resided here in the north for more than half of that time. Anonymously, silently, corresponding with no one except my own conscience. And yet, with each new wind that has blown a ship into our harbor, ever more impossible stories arrive about this creature, Paul, whom I cannot recognize or acknowledge.

They have made me into a legend, almost a god myself. It is their greatest insult. They say, across the communities that revere the risen Yeshua: Paul fought with beasts. Paul was shipwrecked, flogged, stoned, seven times imprisoned. I expect soon to read that Paul conquered a Roman legion single-handed, or rose to the heavens to confer with the Holy One himself, a second Moses -- but perhaps that is going too far. They would only invent such a lie if they had use for it. It is all so far from the man Yeshua, who said "The letter kills, but the spirit gives life."

So many have written about Yeshua, his life and death. The tales are considered as valuable as gold, carefully carried from person to person, decaying scrolls wrapped in leathers and furs, unrolled and recopied time after time, then moved along the furthest roads of the world.

Yeshua is at the center of them all, but hardly recognizable in most. His absence after his crucifixion unleashed a desperate diversity, a continuous unwinding which has not ceased until this day. Have they truly convinced themselves in the writing, in the telling and re-telling? For some he is the triumphant warrior Christ, who will come "in this generation" to save – who? – from – whom? For many, in

Jerusalem and now in Rome, the Jewish covenant with their Holy One has been redrawn as consistent with Yeshua's new covenant, though it could never be so.

I have seen an *Euangelion,* supposedly authored by Yohannon, Yeshua's younger cousin. I have been shown another, by someone calling himself Mark, and another by a Matthias. Could this be that same Matthias, my former friend, tax collector for the high priest? There have been many more, including some allegedly authored by Toma the twin, by young Phillip, and one even claiming Maryam Magdala as its author. Cephas has also supposedly composed a scroll or two, though he was illiterate. Yaakov, equally illiterate, has his own purported *epistolé.*

And just in the past few years, a rash of fresh *epistolés,* ostensibly produced by an apostle named Paul, have begun to appear among the Christians. The first of these emerged from the Asian churches, which were not under the sway of Cephas and James, but followed the young shipmaster Marcion, whose father I knew as a bishop in the city of Sinope, on the shores of the Pontos Euxeinos. I have very little quarrel with the contents of these Marcionite letters: they indict the Jewish Holy One as the *dēmiourgos,* he who is unaware of his limitations, who has forgotten that he is not the highest god, ineffable and unknowable, immanent and transcendent. The Marcionites call this lesser god Ialdabaoth; or Samael, the blind god; or Saklas, the foolish one. They frequently depict him as a serpent with a lion's face. They also allude to the *esoterikos,* the secret message, passed along from initiate to initiate, unrecognizable by the masses.

In addition to the *epistolés* attributed to Paul by Marcion, others have been disseminated in my name. My memory is not what it once was, but when I read them I seem to see familiar words – phrases I spoke or wrote many years ago. These were once brief letters of instruction to this group or that – Corinth, Galatia, Ephesus, Philippi, Thessalonika, Colossae, and even Rome. Littered with redactions and interpolations, they carry the stink of the Jerusalem plotters. I apparently also wrote or dictated several additional *epistolés,* to fictional friends named Titus, Timothy and Philemon. One false *epistolé,* amazingly, is addressed to the entire race of Hebrews.

Lies! Practices and beliefs are described therein that cause me to shiver in despair, even on the warmest day this northland can provide. Hatred of marriage! Denigration of women! Hell-fires that were never spoken of except by the angriest desert prophets! Obedience to and animal fear of the Jewish Holy One! Sometimes I have prayed that Yeshua was indeed a god, if only so that he could return and cast these liars into the pit they have created for others. To my shame.

Recently I received a long narrative that had, by its crumbling appearance, travelled far and been much-handled. Its authorship is attributed to someone named Lukas. This Lukas, an educated Greek, claims to have known me, to have been a traveling companion of mine more than fifty years ago. I have known no Lukas, nor do I see anything of myself in his writings. He appears to be a simpering apologist for Yaakov and Cephas. In his telling, Paul is a minor figure, one who must be criticized and controlled, brought into line, so that the *exoterikos* becomes the only message: judgment and violence and death.

This Lukas is clever. He writes of a miracle that supposedly occurred at the festival of Shevuot in the very year Yeshua was crucified. One morning, according to Lukas, Yeshua's first followers, as well as his mother and other women, were all together in one place in Jerusalem. Suddenly flames appeared over the heads of every one of them; they spoke in strange languages; and thousands of people of all races came up to them and understood their words.

This did not happen, could not have happened. I was still in Jerusalem at the time. It would have been discussed at the Temple, would have been chewed over endlessly in the synagogues, argued on the streets and in every home. The Romans would have taken notice of such a miracle and written of it. At first I was outraged, and then I saw the method to Lukas' cleverness. He wanted to influence Gentiles as well as Jews, and anyone with a Greek education would immediately recognize that the Shevuot scene – now they call it the Pentecost – was appropriated from Euripides' Bachaae, which I saw numerous times in the amphitheater at home in Tarsus. Just as James and Cephas were desperately holding onto their Holy One and his murderous covenant, so Lukas made the story of Yeshua more familiar and therefore more acceptable to those who were not Jews.

Who am I to condemn them, any of them? Here in the North, an old man, I am no longer astonished at what they have done to Yeshua's memory, how they have transformed him in their speeches and in their worship. How they have made him into an idol, a god. How clever they were -- and maybe how callously practical. They had accurately judged the gullibility of the masses, played on fears and hopes, raised themselves up by their former association with Yeshua, the newly deified.

Still, it was brilliant, their re-constituting of my writings. Looking back, I see that it was a kind of compliment. Cephas and his cohort, as they went among the people, making their collections, were no doubt questioned about principles and arguments that I had presented in so many places for so many years. How easy, with me locked away incommunicado, first in Ceasarea Maritima and then in Rome, and finally believed to be dead, for them to elide or add significant phrases, to shade or de-emphasize critical points. At worst, to take the coded words at face value, ignoring Yeshua's hidden true teachings.

All of this pernicious invention, this appropriation of my name and life – all of it stands as nothing, though, compared to the slanders perpetrated against Yeshua. He was a man of excellence, of goodness and kindness. I have not known his like. But he was a man, after all, and not a god. He never said so, never made that claim, whether they shout out to the whole world that he admitted his godhead to each and every last one of them. Liars! Execrable liars!

As a younger man, still on the march, I would become angry, sometimes justifying my anger as had the prophets long ago. Oh, how I wanted to call down fire and brimstone on them. But as I sit here today, an old man, I have learned to bow to the sacred process unfolding. It is not for me to accuse any more, or to rise up even in my heart against their conscious, self-serving inventions. Each new time that Yeshua comes to me, he seems to be cautioning patience. "The Kingdom is at hand, Saul, the Kingdom is at hand." As my early teachers said -- though none of them ever knew Yeshua -- all one has to do is to submit to the endless flow of the world and time.

Yaakov and Cephas-- and their spawn -- could never imagine that necessary step. They submitted to no one, could not free themselves from their Mosaic code. They wanted their Yeshua to be vengeful, they wanted to pay back everyone who had ever harmed or limited their capacious arrogance. The belief that only they were worthy of life and happiness. To them, self-assured of their own righteousness, their Messiah would come – recalibrated as their twisted vision of Yeshua – to destroy. As if they, in their lives, were any better than the least beggar whom they had stepped over each morning on their way to sacrifice blood at their Temple. Or later, when they had accepted their Eucharist, when they sat as mute savages to drink Yeshua's blood and consume his body. They did not hear, apparently, when he spoke of the poor and the meek – though their heirs continue to quote him even today. They only wanted --- they only want – vengeance, pain, validation. Their Christ redeemed them alone, they say.

I do not think so. My continuing visions have led me to this one conclusion: we each redeem ourselves, day by day, when we sit quietly, listen closely to the patterns of the earth and sky, and then diligently set ourselves in accord with those patterns. Love God, he said on the mount. Love all men and all things as if they are God, because God is in all men and all things. The only freedom, then, it becomes clear, is the freedom to love God. As Lucius Annaeus said one afternoon in Rome: *Deus sive natura.* Anything else is error, sacrilege and eventual self-destruction.

At the same time, what spirit is it that comes to me still, seventy-odd years after the Damascus Road? Who never ages, whose voice is as sweet and commanding now as it was then?

Dáire, my friend and patron, has been dead for a generation. I live through the largesse of his son, who is now king in his stead. Cyllin is as tall and broad as Dáire, as fair-haired, and with his own warrior successes. Cyllin honors me as a trusted companion of his father, yet he holds himself at a distance. His eyes cast from side to side, as if he expects me to rise into the air, or suddenly convulse myself into a hideous monster.

I have had a few students over the years. Some time ago, a young man named Theudas arrived and inquired after me by name. He stayed for two years and I shared with him all that I knew. He absorbed what he could about the *dēmiourgos,* the unknown god, and the redemption through grace, the *apolytrisis,* that accompanies faith. I believe that he is in Alexandria now, with an academy of his own.

I am old but have been spared infirmity for the most part. I eat little. My teeth have been gone for many years -- a release from pain for which I give daily thanks. I take long walks -- carefully -- along the precipices that border our island. Breathing the fresh sea air, listening to the calls of seabirds. I also like to wander inland along the narrow paths, watching the sheep grazing behind low stone walls. When I am feeling strong -- though that is a relative term these days -- and when the weather is mild, I climb slowly and soon I am in open fields. Flowers bloom and butterflies move seemingly at random, though I know they are feeding. Tall stone columns, rough and unhewn, stand here like sentinels, reminding me of the holy trees tended by unrepentant Canaanite priestesses, and also of Maryam Magdala's engraved cube. Sometimes I come here to weep.

Here in the north, the rains come with the warm season. But not this year; it has been a dry time. The emerald grasses have turned brown, the winds are hot and heavy. My eyes are not what they once were, so Ailbhe comes each day to read to me.

Ailbhe is of royal blood, Cillin's first child. I remember when she was born, nearly fourteen years ago. Dáire was still alive then, preparing to hand over the chieftain's role. Ailbhe grasped Dáire's finger with her tiny hand, and when she looked at him his eyes lit up as if he had seen eternity. I have said that all the northerners are light-skinned, with straw-yellow hair, but Ailbhe's skin is pure white, and her hair resembles bleached wool. Her face is broad, her cheekbones high. Her brows are straight and dark. Her forceful eyes, so unlike the icy blues and light browns of her people, are as black as the hard stones known in Jerusalem as *achate,* mysterious and incomprehensible. I recall Rebhi Gamaliel saying that the prophet Noah was also white skinned; legends say that Noah's eyes were red. I thought Ailbhe's eyes might be like the *magnes lithos*, which magically attracts metals to itself.

Ailbhe is tall, taller than I am, though I am bowed by age. Her arms and legs are solid, her body capable of great feats of strength, as other children of both genders have often discovered. She moves with the grace and power of a queen. Like many of the women here, she wears at her waist a short sword, lightly and with confidence. She has told me that she is also a skilled archer.

As soon as she could toddle, Ailbhe would find me and ask babbling questions. Although Cillin was doubtful, Dáire directed me to mentor her. Over the years, when she was not busy with the weapons training that all the children, male and female, undertake, Ailbhe would come to me for lessons.

Today, after nearly ten years of study, Ailbhe can read Greek and some Latin, and she has more than a rudimentary understanding of the Jewish law – although, like me, she reads it in the Greek. As my eyesight has dimmed, she has helped me to monitor the many *epistolés* and *euangelia* that appear with disturbing regularity. She is also learning the sorcery and healing arts of this land, passed down primarily through wise women.

The Christians are spreading out across the world, even to this faraway place. Ailbhe asks questions about Yeshua, about Maryam, about Jerusalem before Titus. She asks about his death on the cross, whether he died, and what that may mean.

One morning, Ailbhe settled herself on a thick fur and asked me about life after death.

"What have you been taught?"

She wrinkled her nose.

"The Christian people speak of a judgment," she said slowly. "If you live a good life, you will find a place forever with Yeshua. Is that right?"

"And what if you don't live a good life? Or if you're not perfect?"

"There are two kinds of judgment," she said. "That's what makes it confusing. Some people say that judgment happens after you die – where you go. With Yeshua or with Satan."

"And the second kind?"

"Others say that we are just waiting here for Yeshua to come with angels and destroy this world and all the evil people."

"How do you know if you're evil?"

Her hand found the grip of her sword. I thought of her grandfather Dáire, now dead these past five years.

"If you do bad things?"

I told her the story of Job, as her grandfather Dáire had heard it so many years ago in Rome.

"He was a wealthy man in the old times in Israel," I said, "many many years ago. He had a healthy family, lands and flocks. He sincerely followed all the requirements for worshipping the Jewish Holy One – sacrifice, fasting, prayer."

"What happened to him?"

"The story says that the Holy One was talking with Satan, the dark angel. Satan tempted the Holy One. He said that Job only worshipped because had been given wealth and happiness. So the Holy One took everything away from Job: his health, his lands, his flocks, his family."

"What did Job do?"

"He sat by himself and he mourned, but he still worshipped. Even when the Holy One sent men to challenge his beliefs, he still worshipped properly."

Ailbhe frowned. She tapped her sword-handle.

"What happened to Job?"

"After all that, the Holy One rewarded him with a new family, new flocks, more land."

I paused briefly.

"The lesson that is told about this story is that no matter what happens, you must still worship and obey. And fear. The reward will eventually come to you, in this life or the next."

"I don't think I like this Holy One very much," Ailbhe said. "He is all-powerful, supposedly...

"The creator of heaven and earth, we are told."

"...and yet he could be fooled by Satan into killing Job's innocent family and giving Job illness? I don't think this is a true story."

"It is a story with a lesson."

"What lesson? That their Holy One is less wise than one of my little brothers, who often act out of anger or spite? Here we teach children to act from wisdom and kindness – to grow out of this kind of temper. Don't we?"

Ailbhe's eyes widened in shock.

"I… didn't mean…."

I smiled at her.

"Yes," I said. "You did. This has always been a troubling part of Israel's heritage. The Holy One says many times that he is a jealous god, and this story shows that."

"My mother has told me to live my life courageously," Ailbhe said. "If I believed this story of Job, I would always be in fear – of judgment or even caprice. What if Satan tempts this Holy One and he takes away everything I have? For no reason? What if, unknowing, I make him angry? How will I be judged when I die?"

"My boyhood teachers said that we can either live with courage, moment to moment, or in eternal fear."

Ailbhe resettled herself, wrapping the fur around herself.

"What was Yeshua like?"

"I only met him once in life," I said, "though I saw him die."

She gasped.

"But that is a tale for another day. When I heard him that once, he spoke in a confusing manner. He did speak of judgment, and also of the Kingdom of God, as if sometime soon there would be great destruction, and the Jewish people – believers – would be saved."

"Just as I've heard," Ailbhe said. "Fire and battle and angels and demons."

"I knew a wise woman once -- Maryam Magdala – Yeshua's most trusted friend. She told me that Yeshua had two messages. One for those who could only take a few steps toward wisdom, and a deeper message for those who could hear it, who could bear it all."

"What was that message?"

I rubbed my thinning beard.

"I am still discovering its meaning. But it is not a message of pain and suffering and judgment. He said, 'Those who have ears, let them hear.' I think --- I think he meant that the Kingdom of heaven is inside all of us, all the time, and it is our job during our lives to discover it."

"I have listened," Ailbhe said, "to the old men and women, my father's advisors. They have many different opinions about the god of Israel and Yeshua."

"What do they say?"

"Some say that Yeshua was only a man, but a magician and very wise. Others say he is the son of the Jewish Holy One. Still others say that this Holy One is not the true god, but only a half-god. Who created the heavens and the earth – and all of us who live on the earth, and still is just like a person himself, with emotions and doubts and limits."

"What do you think?"

"If the Jewish Holy One is all-powerful, why is there pain? Why is there death at all? Why is there sadness? If the stories about this Holy One are true, he has created the world just for his amusement, and there must be a higher god."

"Do you think he is evil?"

"I don't know if this Holy One is evil or just ignorant – if he even exists."

"Do you have an answer?"

"In my heart, I feel better when I feel love, when I do good. I feel sad after I am angry or act unfairly to others."

"So you are trying to perfect yourself in love?"

"Yes, but it seems as if living in fear of some ultimate power would not let me act freely... Is there really an angry father-god as in the story you told me, about the man Job?"

"I seem to be returning to my boyhood," I said. "I was taught that there are no gods who interfere and intervene in human lives. Maryam Magdala taught me that this was indeed Yeshua's secret teaching. It has taken me a lifetime to even begin to understand it. And you have found it in your heart without anyone teaching you. Maryam said that living life in love will bring a person to the Kingdom whether the Hebrew stories are true – or if they are not. She said that the age of the Holy One will last until a sufficient number of people have learned to have visions, have discovered their true identities, and have been changed."

"So you were taught then that the Jewish writings are lies?"

"That they were created by men and women of limited wisdom, trying to make sense of their world, and also possessing the deepest fear. I was taught that the idea of god is immanent in what we see as the created world. The heavens, the earth and the sea. People, trees, plants, animals. Everything."

"God is in everything?"

"God is everything. This is what I was taught, both as a boy and by Maryam Magdala."

"And what should people do, then, in their lives?"

"Yeshua said many things about this. I did not understand until years after Maryam explained it to me. 'We must love, she said, 'and in loving all things and all people we can accept that god is in all the world.' Let's look at the Job story from another perspective. Start the same way – with Job as a wealthy, happy good man. Then, because the world is unfolding in time according to its own necessities, all his wealth and happiness are taken from him. What should he do?"

"If he believes that there is only what happens, he should open his heart and accept everything."

"Yeshua spoke of *kenosis*, emptying."

Ailbhe smiled.

"Yes! If Job empties himself of what he thinks should happen – the things he mourns, the things he wants…"

"What he regrets, what he hates…

"If he simply accepts, he will be at peace no matter what happens to him."

I smiled my broadest toothless smile at her.

"And this is what I think Yeshua meant," I said, "when he said that the Kingdom of heaven is always near at hand."

"But this is very different than what is told to the people by the Christian priests."

"I think Yeshua's message persists because it resonates in everyone's heart. As long as there are people alive, his true message exists, is eternal. And at the same time, most people can still live a fair and decent life by following only the rules of the old Hebrew covenant."

"But they are still living in fear, aren't they?"

"We all fear death," I said. "Again, I was taught that overcoming this fear is the beginning of true wisdom. As long as we fear death, we will fear judgment. We will then act well or badly not because we are true to god in our hearts, but because, like children, we fear punishment."

Ailbhe rubbed her chin with a strong thumb and forefinger.

"Yeshua had to leave," she said. "Whether he was a god or a man. Whether the Jewish god sits on a cloud watching us, like an angry chieftain – or whether he does not even exist. Yeshua brought a new idea, didn't he, never presented before? And then he left so that people would have to work it out for themselves. If he had just magically given us wisdom, we would not be wise. We would be intelligent but not wise. Each of us has to obtain wisdom in the working-out of our days."

In summer, I warm my bones in the sun. I see the children running, leaping, laughing at a world newly-discovered. I would like to have been a father: of a strong-limbed boy, climber of trees and city walls, swimmer in churning seas. A boy who would question deeply, speak in calm, measured phrases. Who would lead others to truth.

I would like to have been the father of a girl – though this makes me think I would have had to have a wife. For what could I teach a girl about the wonders of womanhood? About mysteries that no man can ever approach? Perhaps she would have been like Maryam, noble, brilliant as a thousand suns, her blazing core concealed beneath deft arrangements of coiled silk.

I have wondered, at the edge of sleep -- pursued by monsters imagined or real -- whether in all my times with women I have not inadvertently left some trace. Have my sisters, on some long past Tarsan morning, noticed a child at play and recalled -- with a tear or two – their own brother Saul? Has a man come to maturity in Jerusalem, and lived his life without a father to guide him, protect him, or give him comfort?

Maryam said our night of love bore witness to my rebirth, but could there also have been a quickening? Did she bring a child of ours into the world, in some far land where I will never step?

Maryam where are you? The communities of those now calling themselves Christians have spread around the known world, among the Greeks and Romans as well as among the Jews who remain alive.

You said you were going to get a ship at Alexandria, but the Romans killed so many there during those early days. They made no distinction between Christians, Jews or in-betweens. For a time, any worship not directly of the emperor was punishable by death in the arena, burned or on a cross. Did you survive, or were you killed anonymously as so many others?

Did you find, as some have whispered, a cave in Gaul? And do you ever think of me, who loved you so many years ago?

"Tell me about how the world was created," Ailbhe said.

We were sitting on a promontory, facing east back toward the mainland. It was summer, but the air was chill and the sea wind played with her cap of white ringlets.

"You know the story," I said.

She shook her head.

"It's another Hebrew story. I've heard them all my life. He created a man and a woman and they were in a garden. Their life was perfect."

"Do you believe that?"

"They were like children," Ailbhe said. "Or slaves. Who would want to live like that? Slaves have more freedom than they had in that garden. A slave can think about freedom, but their god didn't want them even to do that."

"And then they became curious."

"The woman became curious. I don't know about the man. The serpent came, and told the woman that she could become wise if she ate an apple from a special tree."

"The tree of knowledge."

Ailbhe frowned and sucked at her teeth.

"When they tell this story to children, the serpent is evil."

"But you don't see it that way?"

184

"You have taught me that wisdom comes from living courageously, not in fear. Wasn't the woman being courageous?"

"But she disobeyed."

"She disobeyed a god who told her to be satisfied with what he had given her, and to fear him. In versions of that story that I have heard, this god sounds worried that if the people gain wisdom they will become equal to him. What kind of father is he? My mother and father always tell me to be better than them, stronger, smarter, kinder. Fair to everyone, whether man or woman, free or slave."

"Your parents were also my students, a long time ago."

"And do you want us all to be better than you?"

"Beyond that. None of you would have to do much to be better than me. I have suffered in my life due to ambition, anger and ignorance. It is through all of you that I am finally beginning to see the purpose of my life."

"What does the story mean, then?"

"There is a teaching of fear. As you say, a teaching for children..."

"Or slaves."

"And a teaching for those who crave wisdom so deeply that the craving overcomes the fear."

Ailbhe looked up at the shrill cry of a bird, then followed it with her eyes as it swung on currents of the wind out over the churning sea.

"Two people could hear the same story, then," she said, "in two completely different ways?"

"That was one of the wonders of Yeshua," I said. "Some will hear only a message of submission to authority. For them, the serpent and the woman are evil."

"I don't believe that."

"Only a few – like you -- can hear the message of strength and wisdom."

"The serpent led the woman to wisdom."

"And never forget, she had to have the courage to act."

"What about the man?"

"He had courage also, I think. He loved the woman and he wanted to join her in wisdom, no matter what the cost."

"They were thrown out of that perfect garden," Ailbhe said. "But I would always want to be free, even if I was going to be cold or hungry, rather than be somebody's slave, kept like a pet and in fear."

She grinned at me, then leaped up and raced to the shore, where she casually threw off her robes and dove into the foam. Ailbhe swam in all seasons, riding the black and white wind-blown waves. She often said she would prefer to be a fish, or a dolphin -- a sea-girl. She said she would wrap herself in seaweed, green and brown, and be Queen of all the Oceans. I told her what I had learned as a boy, about the philosopher Anaximander, who said that all humans were originally sea-dwellers. I also told her the legend of Thessalonike, sister of the great Alexander, who was said to have been turned into a mermaid after her death. She would rise from the sea and ask sailors if her brother still lived. If they responded that he was alive, she would calm any storm. If they did not answer correctly, she would raise a tempest, and the ship and all its crew would be drowned.

"Cruel, impulsive and childish," Ailbhe said. "Just like the Jewish Holy One."

By any man's counting, I am very old. I was born in Cilicia in the twenty-sixth year of the great Augustus, and now, far away in Rome, Traianus is in the thirteenth year of his own reign. Yeshua was crucified nearly eighty years ago.

Old enough. I have stopped taking food, although I allow water to pass my lips. Soon I will be no more, unless the Christians are correct and Yeshua awaits, sitting at the right hand of the Holy One. I wonder if I will be welcome, or if I want to be. I am still enough of a student of my first teacher, Cleanthes, to have doubts about any magical, external Kingdom of God. All these years later, I recall him asking: Is there a need for food in Paradise? Where do the rivers empty themselves? Into what sea? Is there a sun to warm a man as he lifts his face in wonder? Are there orchards, heavy with apple, pear or plum? Are the fruits sweet to the taste? Do they never rot on the trees?

But I prevaricate. Forgive me, there is still something I need to say. I have told my small tale without divulging the deepest secret, one that I have carried for all these years like a festering abscess in my heart.

It was another day in Rekem, near the end of my time with Maryam Magdala. We were seated comfortably by a pool on a lower level of her magnificent house. Small golden fish seemed to chase each other in the clear water.

"They have no worries," she said. "See, they swim back and forth, and eat the food which is dropped into their pool."

"But they cannot escape," I said. "They are prisoners of the limited world you have placed them in."

Maryam cast a piercing glance at me. She knew me better than I knew myself.

"What is it, Saul?"

"What happened on the night he was taken? You have never told me."

Maryam cast her head down, pausing for so long that I thought she did not intend to answer me.

"We were gathered in Gethsemane near the foot of the Mount of Olives," she said at last, in a soft voice with her eyes downcast. "It was here that so many Jews were buried, in caves and in marble coffins laid on the hard, dry ground. I stood apart with some of the women, including Yeshua's mother. The men were arguing, as men do. Only Yeshua seemed calm. Yaakov, his brother, stood alone as was his habit, saying nothing but watching everyone and everything. Cephas, always a firebrand, was trying to whip the men into a fury of revolt against the Romans. Shimon, whom we called Zelotes, shouted even louder than Cephas, hurled greater curses at the occupiers. I thought that

Cephas' fire came not from rage but from fear – fear that of all the former followers of Yohannon the Baptizer, now wandering like lost sheep, it was Yeshua and not him that the people were beginning to listen to. At first, Cephas cleverly avoided direct criticisms of Yeshua, but it was clear that he was trying to influence the group away from words of peace and love. He appeared to agree with Shimon's fulminations, but I noticed that he was just a bit less volatile, just a bit more conciliatory. He masterfully undercut Shimon – or else Shimon was his willing accomplice, carrying the men to higher pitches of emotion so that Cephas could appear to be the more reasonable one. The men looked anxiously at Yeshua, who remained silent. Finally, Cephas approached Yeshua.

"What do you think, now that you are the voice of the people? Should we fight like men, or run like children?"

"If we fight, Cephas, we will forfeit our lives, as so many have."

"Do you think that the Romans are not men, like we are, that they cannot die?"

"All men die. But there must be a purpose both to life and to death."

Cephas waved his arms in frustration. Shimon and one or two others nodded in agreement.

"Is not a glorious death in battle a great enough purpose for you?"

Yeshua gestured toward us, by now huddled together anxiously. He glanced at his brother Yaakov, then his gaze passed back to Cephas.

"And what of them, those who cannot fight? Will the Romans spare them, after you have fallen? You all know their ways; they will take them and either kill them or make them slaves."

Cephas sneered.

"And what would you do, who are now called King of the Jews?"

Yeshua closed his eyes and was silent for a moment. His face hardened.

"I never asked for that title."

Cephas grabbed Yeshua"s arm.

"But what would you do? What will you order us to do, we who are mere witnesses to your greatness?"

Yeshua did not answer him.

Cephas' eyes gleamed. He looked around at all of us.

"Here stands the King of the Jews. Some even call him the Messiah, come to rescue us from these invaders."

"Come to fulfill prophecy," said Shimon.

Cephas stood back and crossed his arms. Then he stooped and picked up a pebble.

"Well, Messiah," he said, "if you are so powerful, turn this stone into bread. We are hungry, for we have eaten little today."

Yeshua remained silent, his face blank and empty.

Cephas pointed toward the west, where the uppermost parts of the Temple could just be seen.

"It is written that the Messiah will go to the highest place, and from there, he will throw himself down, and angels will catch him and will raise him up. Why don't you go to the Temple, Yeshua, and throw yourself down? Then we will all bend our knees before you."

I didn't notice at the time, but that must have been when Yehudah, from the town of Kerioth, stole away into the night. Cephas had one last insult. He stood back and addressed us all.

"If Yeshua is the Messiah," he said, "let him go up onto this Mount of Olives, to the highest peak, and let him look down on all the kingdoms of the world, even as far as Rome, and declare that he is the ruler over all."

Yeshua still did not respond. Yaakov seemed to be studying Cephas very closely.

"King of the Jews," Cephas said. He spat at Yeshua's feet. "King of the Jews!"

He then turned and walked forcefully out of the garden. The other men glanced hesitantly at Yeshua. When he did not move or acknowledge them, they too left. Yaakov was the last to leave.

Yeshua walked over to those of us who remained at the edge of the garden.

"I have no advice, he said, save what I have said before. Love one another. Go now, all of you. I fear it will soon become dangerous to be out in the night."

"The next morning, we heard that he had been taken by the Roman soldiers, led to the spot by Yehudah. My first thought at the time was that Yehudah was Cephas' most faithful follower, always available to do Cephas' bidding."

I leaped to my feet.

"They betrayed him!"

Maryam stood, came very close to me, and stared into my eyes.

"There is more."

She reached for my hands and drew me down next to her.

"After they took him off the cross," she said, "I followed them into Joseph's house, and together Joseph and I slowly healed him of his wounds. It took more than thirty days, nearer to forty, before he was able to walk without effort, even for a little while. He was painfully thin and still weak. His wounds had begun to heal, though we still changed his bandages twice each day and applied poultices. We could not entice him to eat much, but he took both water and wine."

Maryam frowned. Lines formed at the edges of her mouth and between her firm brows.

"By then, as you know, they had begun saying that he had risen from the mountain top, carried off to heaven in the company of Elijah and Moses."

The lines around her face tightened.

"I only know that what I saw was a man. A man at the very edge of death, fragile and nearly broken."

Maryam stood so suddenly that I thought she would fall over. Her face went white, and then she regained herself and sat down again next to me.

"You were at his crucifixion, as you have said. You saw that his so-called friends and brothers, even his actual brother, were too cowardly to appear."

"But they were wanted men, weren't they?"

"Wanted men? If they were wanted men, the Romans would have given them crosses of their own. You saw for yourself, there was plenty of wood. Golgotha was a city of crosses, and hanging on each one was a man, dead or dying. Birds picked at rotting corpses, their triumphant cries overcoming the screams of agony and the final laboring gasps."

"Cowards," I said.

"They were unimportant. Small men, of no consequence. We knew that Cephas and Yaakov and the others were continuing to meet at the spot where Yeshua had been taken. Gethsemane. It had been a frequent gathering place, and they had nothing to fear. Joseph and Nicodemus had told no one what we had done. Rome lost interest after what they believed was Yeshua's death. The Sadducees were no longer threatened by Yeshua reminding the people that they were traitors, agents of Rome and their own greed."

"The natural order was resumed."

Maryam wrung her hands together.

"He was determined to show himself. He thought his followers would be joyous, their brother returned. We walked together to Gethsemane and he showed himself. Only Matthias and young Yohannon were absent. And the women."

"Were they not overjoyed?"

"I don't know who it was, Cephas or more likely Yaakov, so noble in his filthy robe and his unshorn hair. One of them quickly realized that Yeshua could be more useful if he remained a martyr."

Maryam's gentle face assumed for a moment a deep bitterness.

"They crowded around him, asked to see his wounds, touched him."

"And then...?"

"And then you could see them begin to calculate. I saw the light dawn in Yaakov's eyes. His loving brother, alive, was in the way of Yaakov's glorious plans. What if Yeshua returned to show the people he had survived? Wouldn't that make things even more dangerous for Yaakov, Cephas and the others, whom the Romans had clearly forgotten? At the very least, what if Yeshua continued to promote his message of love? Wouldn't it undermine their own primacy with the people?"

A tear slid down Maryam's cheek.

"It was his own brother who drew the first blade, who made the first thrust. Yaakov's purity apparently allowed fratricide. Remember, according to their thinking, Yeshua was King of the Jews, of the line of David. If Yeshua was King, only a member of his family could succeed him. Not Cephas, but Yaakov. Only Yaakov."

"What did you do?"

Maryam drew a breath so thin and sharp that she nearly hissed.

"My people stood ready," she said, "but that was not Yeshua's way. He looked into my eyes one last time, and then forgave them as he died. When he lay there with his robes rent, his blood leaking out into the dirt, Yaakov sidled up to me. How he stank, his unwashed holiness."

"Now my brother is truly gone," he said. "We will hide him well, Maryam, in a cave on the Mount of Olives. We will continue to say that we have seen him. We will say that God has exalted and glorified him. We will say that he has defeated death and ascended from the Mount of Olives, until he comes again as the true Messiah. "

When, I was a boy in Tarsus, I asked Cleanthes if my visions were real or true. He answered with a question.

"What does it matter, Saul? If they affect you, frighten you or illuminate the world for you, what does their physical truth or reality matter?"

Cleanthes saw my hesitation and confusion. He came close and put a hand on my shoulder, as I have done so many times in my life with quaking penitents and seekers.

"Can you prove to me that I am real, young Saul?"

This was a lesson presented to the younger boys almost as soon as they entered the academy. I admitted that I could not.

"Then you are limited to your awareness of yourself and the world around you. But you have a rational intuition – *noesis* -- that these are, as you say, real and true.*"

I nodded.

"Are your dreams and so-called visions provable as any less or more real than I am -- or your mother, or your sisters?"

I had to admit that they were not.

"Then, Saul, this follows the many conversations we have had on the truth or reality of the gods. We trust that they are real and true as ideas, and we can calmly observe them, study them, and be influenced by them, without asking unnecessary metaphysical questions. "

I recall this teaching, offered nearly a century ago, whenever I hear the Christians' arguments about Yeshua's bodily resurrection. Maryam Magdala said that Yeshua was killed by his friends and followers. By his brother. If I do not doubt her – and I do not – then the assassins knew there would be no resurrection of his body. They knew that they hid him – broken and forgotten -- on the Mount of Olives. Yeshua's elevation to heaven is nothing more than a cold and cynical appropriation. The plotters assimilated old tales of Enoch and Elijah, who were believed to have gone to *Pardes* while alive, and who were waiting for the messianic times, when they would return to earth.

Of course, after all these years, it now appears that there were multitudes who saw the risen Yeshua -- or as they call him, the Christ. Some even have claimed to have touched him, although Maryam said that he would not allow even her to embrace him in that brief interval between the cross and the assassins' knives.

I sometimes wonder if they bothered to wrap him in a shroud after they killed him – Cephas was always in a hurry -- or whether they just tossed him into a convenient cave before slinking away to infamy.

But after all, Cleanthes – and Maryam -- were right. It doesn't matter. Yeshua -- my visions of him, my knowledge of him -- will remain true as long as I am alive. And I am not special; if I can experience Yeshua, anyone can. Whenever one person reaches into his – or her – heart, Yeshua will remain resurrected, no matter if people quarrel over his unfound desiccated bones for thousands of years.

I am tired. I have been tired for so long. Energy and passion have been siphoned out of me through decades of interminable arguing. And the lies: the self-serving fantasies which seem to be multiplying like dung beetles after a herd of cows has passed.

Oh, the dances they have done in their minds, the tortured paths their words have taken so that they could remake Yeshua into their private avenging angel, coming to destroy everyone but them. They knew him in his earthly form but never as the living Christ -- though I have heard that Cephas eventually made that claim. They garbled his words – as have so many others! – their own limited ideas and opinions seeping like foul mud into the garden of truth.

Nevertheless, they have won, the Jerusalem Jews; those Nazarenes, those Christians. Most of them are now as dead as their precious holy city and their Temple, but their writings remain, like shards of broken pottery thrown into a side-yard for future generations to ponder. They have forced new words into Yeshua's mouth, made him say things that were never said. Already, many if not most who speak of Yeshua have rendered him a kind of Greek god, warrior son of the Jewish Holy One. I wonder, if this process continues, what future men and women will think of the good man Yeshua and those who travelled with him. But maybe it is that I am only a child of my time, unable to see the working-out of things, unable to gain the rarified heights experienced by Yeshua and Maryam.

My strength diminishes. It will not be long now. Each day it is harder to believe that Yeshua's true message still courses through this dismal world, an underground stream bubbling up from a pure infinite source. I wonder if Maryam, somewhere, has attained the wisdom she hoped for. I know that I have not.   I still hold onto petty grievances and regrets, still have desires – although these are generally desires of impatience. Things do not move fast enough for me. I would like to know the Kingdom, and I have run out of time.